DEATH AND DACQUOISE

A SEASIDE FRENCH PATISSERIE MYSTERY
BOOK 1

KAT BELLEMORE

KB PRESS

CHOOSE YOUR OWN ADVENTURE: MYSTERY OR ROMANCE

MADDIE SWALLOWS MYSTERIES:

New Mexican Cozy Mystery

Dead Before Dinner

Dead Upon Arrival

Dead Before I Do

Dead Among Stars

Dead by Design

Dead in the Dark

Dead Without a Hitch

SEASIDE FRENCH PATISSERIE MYSTERIES

Death and Dacquoise

Poison and Pudding

BORROWING AMOR: New Mexican Romance

Borrowing Amor

Borrowing Love

Borrowing a Fiancé

Borrowing a Billionaire

Borrowing Kisses

Borrowing Second Chances

STARLIGHT RIDGE: Beach Romance

Diving into Love

Resisting Love

Starlight Love

Building on Love

Winning his Love

Returning to Love

Fearless Love

1

They said that owning your own business could be the most rewarding thing you had done in your life. It provided freedom and independence—a sense that you had put something out into the world that was uniquely yours.

Now that I thought about it, I couldn't remember who had told me that. It was probably on an ad for one of those self-promoting 'success' gurus, trying to pump me up so they could sell me their book.

Had I dived a little deeper into what my sister and I were getting ourselves into, I would have maybe found someone who was a little more honest. Someone who would tell me about the anxiety, frustration, and ever-present self-doubt. None of which was healthy for a sixty-eight-year-old heart like mine. By agreeing to open a bakery at my age, I was fairly certain I'd taken a few years off my life.

It had definitely taken off more than a few for my sister, Dottie, and she was older than I was. The previous evening, I had casually asked if she had drawn up a will yet and if I was in it. She hadn't liked that much—me thinking about her future demise—and she never answered me.

"Just a little more to the right," I yelled, squinting against the sun as I watched our store sign being lowered into place.

It was glorious.

The most brilliant blue and gold you could imagine.

Sandcastle Bakery, it read, complete with a small gold sandcastle above the name.

In this moment, it all seemed worth it—the anxiety and frustration of the past few months were long forgotten when I saw that sign and realized this was really happening. All those months of wondering if we could really pull this off—Dottie and I were opening a bakery.

Maybe those so-called gurus knew a little something after all.

When trying to decide what to name our store, there hadn't really been a decision to be made. Our eldest sister, Beatrice, had died last year, and in a moment of pure insanity, Dottie and I had abandoned our lives elsewhere —to be fair, they hadn't been all that great—and moved to this little Californian seaside community that our sister had loved so much.

I suppose saying Beatrice had died was the polite way of putting it.

She had been murdered.

A seventy-four-year-old former CIA analyst who had been slowly losing her sanity amid her paranoia that the government was watching everything she did.

Who knew, she might not have been far off.

Her downward spiral had slowed when she'd moved to this wonderful town, Starlight Ridge, and turned an old bakery into a souvenir shop. She'd named it Sandcastle Souvenirs, and she'd sold healing crystals and tarot cards alongside the standard tourist T-shirts, while also baking bread in the back for anyone who might want some. Not exactly your typical souvenir shop.

Dottie and I—we were of course going to pay tribute to her when we took over her store. But that didn't mean we wanted to continue selling discounted souvenirs that our sister had bought on clearance.

And so, Sandcastle Bakery had been born.

The store door opened, and I glanced over just as Dottie's cat, Skittles, zoomed past my sister. Dottie tripped over Skittles and caught herself on the open door. She placed a hand on her hip and shook her head. "That cat was an inside cat until I moved here."

"Everyone is an inside everything where you come from," I said with a laugh. "Up north, it's too cold to be outside."

"I suppose that's true." She leaned against the open

door, catching her breath. "You changed your hair again. I'm not a fan of the green. I prefer the pink."

Yes, I knew. Dottie had always had an opinion about my hair color, but sometimes I liked to experiment a little and try new things. I had to agree with her, though. The green hadn't turned out quite like I'd expected, and it looked like someone had thrown up all over my head. I'd fix that this afternoon, though. No harm done.

"Thank you for your feedback. I'll take it into consideration," I said, then refocused my attention on the sign, squinting and tilting my head, looking for any evidence it was crooked. I glanced back at Dottie. I hated what age had done to my sister, and it pained me to see her this way.

"You sign up for that yoga class yet?" I asked. "I hear that Beatrice went at least two or three days a week, and she'd never been healthier."

Dottie scowled. "Yes, that's what I've heard too. A gimmick to try to get me to buy a monthly membership."

I laughed. "You're saying that the proven health benefits of yoga are a gimmick?"

Skittles ran through my legs, her tail sweeping them as she went, and she looked up at me and meowed.

"Skittles is saying that you're a hypocrite," Dottie said, joining us. "You've never done yoga a day in your life."

That was true. I didn't have the patience for it.

"That's because I'm starting parkour on Friday," I said, stealing a glance at my sister. "It's a bit more my speed."

Her lips parted but no words came out—just the sort of reaction I'd been hoping for.

And then Dottie laughed. A lot. Certainly more than necessary.

"You are doing parkour? Don't they have an age limit for that sort of thing?"

I jutted out my chin, not appreciating her mockery. "Anyone of any age can do it. Will I be leaping off buildings? Probably not. We'll see. But it's supposed to have many of the same benefits as yoga. I'll have better balance, reaction time, strength—everything I want and have been lacking. All without having to be flexible and hold the stupid position until I either give up or die."

Dottie considered me for a moment. "You're going to kill yourself. You know that, right? Probably within the first lesson."

"You could always join me and keep me from dying."

I'd known she wouldn't go for it, but it was always worth a try.

Dottie frowned. She'd been doing that a lot lately. Before Beatrice had died, Dottie and I hadn't seen each other in seven years. When we'd decided to both start over and move to Starlight Ridge, everything had become brighter.

We had needed each other. And new friends. And the ocean. And the sun.

A purpose.

But for the past month or two, the closer we'd gotten to

the grand opening of our bakery, the deeper Dottie had seemed to have fallen into a hopelessness that I didn't know how to help her out of.

"You know that I can't do parkour, or yoga, or anything else that requires me to put weight on my knees," Dottie finally said. "You mean well, but I've been traveling down this slippery slope for a long time now, and there's no turning back. Unless you have a time machine, this is my new reality."

That was when I realized what this was. Her mood over the past couple of months—it wasn't about the grand opening.

"Your seventieth birthday," I said, realization dawning on me. "You're entering a new decade. That's what this is all about."

We had planned on having a giant seventieth birthday party for Dottie on the same day as the grand opening. I say 'we', but really, it had been my idea, and Dottie had merely gone along with it. The plan was to invite everyone in town to the party, serve food from the bakery as dessert, and give everyone a taste of what we had to offer.

Voila. Instant customers.

Dottie had never said anything against the plan, but now that I thought about it, she had been awfully quiet about it. Too quiet.

Even now, she gave me a long look before releasing a sigh. "There's that saying that we're not getting any younger. But I'm afraid that as I grow older, that trajectory is becoming exponential. What am I doing opening a bakery at my age? It's ludicrous."

I understood her sentiment—I had had similar thoughts.

I took Dottie's hands in mine, and her gaze found me. "Dorothy, you can use what's left of your life to wallow and feel sorry for yourself, or you can go on this grand adventure. You probably still have two decades left to explore and invent and imagine. Wouldn't you rather do that with me and enjoy the time you have left? Yes, I might kill myself doing parkour, or learning how to scuba dive, or heck, I might actually break down and learn how to use all that fancy baking machinery we have in the back of the store. But whatever I do, it's going to be on my own terms."

I didn't usually speak with Dottie in this way, and I certainly never called her by her given name, but desperate times called for desperate measures. I was worried I had gone too far, though, and I held my breath.

Dottie stared for a beat longer than made me comfortable, and then she nodded. "All right. We'll have the biggest seventieth birthday party this town has ever seen. We'll open up this crazy bakery that only serves French desserts because we don't know how to bake and the woman we hired learned everything she knows in Paris. And I'll go to parkour with you." My immediate excitement must have been obvious, because she held up a finger. "But only to make sure you don't die. I'm not planning on participating."

I grinned, not believing my luck, and clapped my hands together. "Ooh, we're going to have so much fun. Autumn is the one who introduced me to what parkour even is. It will be like a team bonding experience every Friday."

Dottie's smile disappeared. "If we're all at parkour every Friday, who's going to be watching the store?"

I hadn't thought that far.

Autumn was our only employee, but she was more important to the bakery than Dottie and me combined.

The fact that she only knew how to bake fancy French desserts didn't matter; it was what set us apart from everyone else. If there had been anyone else. There was one woman in town, Jessie, who baked out of her kitchen, but she was mostly retired and baked for fun, so I didn't count her as competition.

"We're a French patisserie," I told Dottie in my best upper-class voice. "We close up and take those fancy midday naps that are all the rage in Europe."

Dottie snorted. "That's a siesta, and they do it in Latin America. Besides, they use it to sleep, not work harder."

"They have them in Greece too," I said. "I'm sure of it. It was on a documentary I once watched."

I was saved from having to further defend myself when Erwin, the owner of the Seaside Bay restaurant, walked past us with his golden retriever.

"Jo is right," he said. "They take midday naps in Greece. But you don't need to use them for an excuse. If no one is in the restaurant, I lock up and put a sign on the door saying I'll be back in an hour, and I give my cooking staff a break."

Dottie and I shared confused expressions.

"People don't care that they show up and you are randomly closed?" I asked.

Erwin raised a shoulder. "They'll return if they're hungry. Besides, it's not a big town. If it's that important, they'll find me."

I looked to Dottie with a satisfied grin. I'd never seen a company be successful with that kind of business model, but if Erwin said that was how it was done here, I had no trouble adapting.

And taking breaks whenever I felt like it was certainly something I could adapt to.

Dottie didn't seem as convinced, but she nodded. "All right. Parkour Fridays it is."

I looked back to the store, the sign now installed, and I felt a deep sense of pride. I understood Dottie's anxiety. Neither of us had done anything this crazy—this risky.

I liked to think we were doing it for Beatrice.

2

Twelve hours until the big event, and I wasn't feeling remotely prepared. I'd told Dottie she wasn't allowed to decorate for her own party, but I should have swallowed my pride and at least asked for help blowing up these balloons. I didn't have the lung capacity, or the oxygen, that I used to. So far, I had exactly four inflated balloons, and I was already lightheaded. Balloons were one of those things you needed a lot of or none at all, but four balloons would just make our party look sad. Like we had tried but had obviously failed.

"Jo, you around?" I heard Autumn call from the front door, right before a loud POP and a scream.

Now we were down to three balloons, thanks to Skittles, who had decided to sneak attack one of them.

I poked my head up from behind the counter, where I'd sat on the floor for a break. "Right here."

Autumn yelped again, startled by my presence, then placed a hand over her chest, laughing. "We really need to get some stools for behind there."

"They were supposed to arrive yesterday, but there's been a delay," I said. "You people really need to work on your mail delivery system here."

Autumn raised a shoulder, as if to say, *What are you going to do about it?*

"We're too far out of the way here," she said. "We get deliveries twice a week. If your order is delayed by a day, that means you most likely won't get it for three or four. And that's if Gerald remembers to bring it to you once it's delivered to the post office. With just him running the place, things tend to fall through the cracks."

So I had been warned.

"Well, I know how you can make it up to me," I said, attempting to stand. My body wasn't having any of it, however, and I held up a hand, waving it so Autumn would get the hint that I needed help up. I was okay using body language to convey my needs, but I was too proud to actually ask.

Autumn walked over, took my hand, and pulled me up so fast, I nearly body slammed her.

"Girl, you need to stop working out. You're getting too strong."

"It's your fault," she said. "I've been baking nonstop getting ready for tonight, and I'm starting to see my muscles again." Autumn picked up the bag of balloons off the counter and got to work blowing them up.

"Speaking of baking," I said with a crooked smile, "I think you should let me taste test what you've made for tonight. Security reasons, you understand."

Autumn laughed, but then her smile dipped, and she absentmindedly pulled on a balloon, as if getting ready to blow it up, but then she never did. "Here's the thing," she said. "You hired me based on my reputation without ever giving me a proper interview or anything, and then you approved the menu for tonight with barely a glance. Don't get me wrong, I'm grateful for the opportunity. But French desserts—you are familiar with éclairs, macarons, and that kind of thing. And I've made plenty of those. But what I really loved baking when I was in France were the things that not many have heard of. Things like dacquoise and madeleines."

I blinked. "I'm sorry...duh...what?"

Her lips tilted up at the corners. "You pronounce it da-kwaaz, though half those cooking shows on TV say it wrong. There are endless varieties, but I've always liked it with hazelnut meringue layered with cream and strawberries. I went ahead and made some for tonight—I hope you don't mind."

My mouth was already watering at the thought of it. "I don't think you can ever go wrong with hazelnut and strawberries." I paused and took the balloon from her. "I'm sorry if we haven't given the menu much attention. You see, Dottie and I, well, we didn't realize how much went into opening a store, let alone throwing a birthday party that doubles as a grand opening—a party that we've invited the entire town to. We've been so worried about the logistics that I figured I'd just let you handle where your expertise lay. I can be a more hands-on kind of boss if you like."

Autumn smiled, grabbed some tape, and started securing the balloons along the folding tables we'd set up. "You can be any kind of boss you want to be, and of course, I'm happy to let you taste test everything. I just wanted to make sure you knew what you'd gotten yourself into."

I hadn't known what I had gotten myself into for six months now. But at this point, it was a little too late to worry about something like that.

I just hoped people showed up tonight, or we were going to have a lot of duhkah on our hands...or whatever it was called. Maybe I'd just call it meringue cake.

THREE HOURS LATER, I was exhausted, but the bakery was decorated. I leaned against the wall, and Skittles walked up, rubbing against my leg. She was begging to be petted, but that would require bending over, and I didn't have it in me. Autumn was kind enough to fetch a couple of folding chairs from the back room, and I collapsed into one. I should have let Dottie help. Several other people in town had offered as well, but then I'd be allowing a guest to decorate for a party they'd been invited to, and that wasn't any better. The only reason I felt okay about Autumn helping was because I was paying her.

And now I was paying for my stubbornness with swollen feet and aching fingers.

"At least we have the afternoon to relax," I said. "I need a nap."

Skittles was already halfway there, having leaped onto my lap the moment I'd sat down. I didn't see why she felt the need to sleep—the only thing she'd done as we'd decorated was make more work for us, attacking anything that might move. The streamers had been the worst. Hopefully the guests wouldn't look too closely, because they'd find claw marks in several of them.

Dottie appeared at that moment, walking in from the back entrance, and drew in a sharp breath. "This looks amazing." She glanced at me. "Seriously, Jo. You didn't need to go to so much trouble. People would have been fine with just a banner and—"

"And you're saying you don't think you were worth all this trouble," I interrupted. "But you are, and you were. So, you might as well enjoy it."

She smiled. "Thank you, Jo and Autumn. It's beautiful, and everyone is going to have a lovely time tonight."

I stretched against the back of the chair, my arms high above my head. "If anyone needs me, I'll be upstairs and —" I paused when I realized Dottie had changed into a bright pink and green tracksuit. I hadn't even known she owned exercise clothes, let alone that she'd actually wear them. These looked like they were straight out of the nineties.

"What is that?" I asked, gesturing to her outfit.

Dottie glanced down, her cheeks reddening like she was embarrassed. "Do you like it?" Her eyes begged for approval.

Autumn looked like she was trying to hold in a laugh, and she turned away in an attempt to hide her smile.

"I do," I said slowly, wanting to support my sister, because it was obvious she had gone to a lot of effort for it. "But why are you wearing it?"

"Doesn't parkour start in thirty minutes?" she asked, confused.

I didn't respond right away, mostly because I had forgotten it was Friday and had certainly not expected to attend our first class on the same day as Dottie's big party-slash-grand opening.

But then I saw Dottie's expression. The disappointment that lay there when she realized I hadn't planned on going—it broke my heart. For all of her complaining about being dragged along, she had actually been looking forward to it. Even bought an outfit she'd deemed appropriate for the occasion.

"Oh," she said, her voice soft. "We're not going. That's all right. I'm sure you're tired from all the work you've put in this morning. I'll just go back upstairs and change and—"

"Absolutely not," I said, standing up and forgetting I had a cat on my lap. Skittles flew off, landed on her feet, then narrowed her eyes before sauntering away and curling up on the floor in the middle of a sun spot. "We're going to class. I just had to rest my feet for a moment or two. And now they are rested, so I will change, and we will go to parkour class. That starts in thirty minutes." I glanced at Autumn. "All of us."

Autumn was no longer smiling, but she understood that this was non-negotiable. "I'll run home and change, then be back in fifteen minutes to pick you two up," she said.

Dottie gave me a hesitant smile. "Are you sure you're up to it? We can always plan on next week—"

"I'm already on my way to change," I said, walking toward the back of the store.

I paused at the bottom of the stairs.

As grateful as I was that we could live in the small apartment above the bakery, those stairs were my nemesis, and I might need an extra-long nap after climbing them.

But I couldn't allow myself to give in to temptation, because today was Dottie's birthday. She could tell we hadn't planned on attending parkour today and that we were doing it because we felt bad. And that wasn't how I wanted today to go for Dottie. So, I threw on my widest smile, retrieved my exercise pants and a T-shirt, laced up my tennis shoes, and pretended that I believed I might come out of this alive.

3

T he closer we drove to the beach, the more nervous I got. Maybe this had been a mistake. But despite Dottie's initial protests, she was excited, and it was the first time I'd seen that excitement in several months. There was no backing out of it now.

"So...no jumping off buildings, right?" I asked, hoping my shaking voice would be taken as a sign of age and not nervousness.

Autumn laughed. "No buildings. I have extreme anxiety about...well, everything...and they've been really good about not pushing me beyond my comfort level. I know the YouTube videos make it seem like parkour is this crazy extreme thing, but it's really about mastery of your body and using your environment to stay active."

"Mastery of my body," Dottie mused. "That sounds

nice. Not sure how much they can do with what I've got, though."

We pulled into a parking space at the boardwalk, and Autumn glanced at us. "Seriously, don't compare yourself to what other people are doing. You shouldn't expect yourself to do what the twenty-year-olds are doing."

"I don't think I'll have a problem with that," I said, chuckling. "Now, not comparing myself to the fifty-year-olds, that will be tougher."

Not that I expected there to be anyone even close to my and Dottie's ages.

So, of course, the first person we saw was Jessie, the matriarch of the town. She was only a few years younger than me, but, in addition to being famous for the tarts she baked, she was athletic and strong. When I'd first met her, she had been scooping me off the pavement because I'd fallen from a bike. And the bike hadn't even been moving when I fell. I would definitely be comparing myself to her.

As we approached, I knew the moment Jessie had noticed us. With a squeal, she hurried over to us and wrapped both Dottie and me in a tight group hug.

"Autumn said you'd be joining us. I just didn't realize it would be so soon. You are going to love this class." She ushered us forward. "Let me introduce you to the instructor."

When I had imagined the instructor, I had expected one of those twenty-something-year-olds that Autumn had warned us not to compare ourselves to. Instead, a man who looked around sixty turned and gave us a megawatt smile. Seriously, he was gorgeous. And those brown eyes. I generally preferred green, but they were certainly something I could get used to. It left me wondering why I'd never noticed him around town before.

My feet suddenly weren't hurting from standing all morning, and my back no longer ached. This class was already providing health benefits, and we hadn't actually done anything yet.

"Hi, I'm David," he said, extending a hand.

I stared.

Dottie nudged me, then took the outstretched hand. "I'm Dorothy, and this is Josephine."

That snapped me out of my stupor.

"Jo, actually," I said, shooting Dottie a glare. She knew I hated my full name. "My friends call me Jo."

I wanted to shake his hand too, but once Dottie released it, it wasn't offered to me.

"Nice to meet you, Dorothy and Jo." And then David began explaining what our first day of class would look like.

Darn that Dottie, wanting the instructor all for herself.

"He's why most of us show up to class," Jessie murmured. "Can you believe he's sixty-eight? He looks at least a decade younger."

No, I couldn't believe it. But when I glanced around, I realized that the class disproportionately consisted of older women. Sure, there were plenty of younger men and women, but there were far more in my age bracket than would be normal for a class like this.

I'd just joined Starlight Ridge's version of senior aerobics. And everyone was hot for the teacher.

Another nudge from Dottie.

"Would you feel comfortable with that?" David was asking me.

I was unsure what the first part of the question had been, but I had a feeling that whatever it had been, the answer was "Yes."

David seemed surprised. "Really? That's wonderful. Autumn told me you were adventurous."

I threw Dottie a panicked gaze, my eyes begging her to tell me what I'd just agreed to.

She only laughed at me.

"We're going to do some quick introductions while we warm up, then we'll get to the good stuff," he said, motioning for us to follow him.

"You're so lucky," Jessie told me. "It took me a while to get comfortable with parkour, but once I started doing the balance bar regularly, it's made all the difference."

Oh, no. If the balance bar was anything like I'd seen in competitive gymnastics, Dottie was right. I was going to die.

We joined the rest of the class, about fifteen of us in total, and began winding our arms like windmills. Apparently, my windmill was a bit rusty, because the fans didn't turn like they used to, only making it about halfway around.

"We have two new members today," David told the others. "Jo and Dorothy." He pointed to a young man next to him. "This is Peter, one of our assistant coaches. He works with our more experienced students." Peter stood in a solemn stance, his arms folded, and gave us a nod. His muscles weren't as toned as our instructor's, and he was a little on the overweight side, which surprised me, but he looked like he made up for it in determination. His long hair was held back with a bandana, and his expression told me he was ready for anything.

David then pointed to a young woman next to him who had the athletic build I expected from someone in a parkour class, her hair pulled up into a ponytail and an easy smile on her face.

"This is Eliza. She's my other assistant coach and will be working with the beginners. I will be bouncing between the two groups as needed. It's up to you to determine where you belong, because only you know your skill level. As we progress through the classes, I may provide some guidance, but that's all it is. This class is yours. Take ownership. And when I say that, I mean take ownership of your life. Of your health. In this class, there is no room for excuses, only progression. And of course, please don't take yourselves too seriously. I expect you to have fun. No one is good at this stuff their first time trying it. The more you laugh at yourself while you do it, the better you'll become."

Eliza cleared her throat and raised her hand.

He smirked. "Okay, almost no one gets it their first try. Eliza here is an exception. But not all of us are blessed with her innate athletic prowess."

David was one heck of a motivational speaker. All my anxiety dissipated, and I was left with nothing but excitement and determination to take control of my life and live up to his expectations. In that moment, if he'd asked me to run three miles along the beach, I would have. Of course, I'd have collapsed a few yards into it, but I would certainly have given it my all.

As it turned out, what he did ask of us was much more difficult than I had expected. And that was just for the warmup. He had us bouncing on our toes, balancing on one foot, then the other. By the end of the five-minute warmup, I was ready to go home.

Unfortunately, there were another fifty-five minutes that I'd committed to, and I couldn't very well back out now. Not after all that talk about taking control of our lives and not offering any more excuses.

Even if that commitment did include a balance bar that was likely to kill me. Unfortunately, like Dottie, I hadn't drawn up a will. At least, that was what I'd assumed her silence had meant when I'd asked. I wondered if there was a lawyer in town who could help us out with that.

"Beginners over here," David called, gesturing to Eliza. "Advanced students over there with Peter."

I didn't recognize most of the people in the class, but I

did recognize Isaac, the local lifeguard. He was in his early twenties, and he immediately joined Peter. No surprise there. Jessie joined Eliza with the other older women. It seemed that labeling the groups 'beginner' and 'advanced' was just a nice way of separating us by 'old' and 'young.'

David gestured to Dottie and me. "Which group would you two like to try out today?"

There was no question which one we belonged in, but I thought it would be polite to confer with Dottie first. She'd stood on the periphery of the group during warmups, leaning on her cane. I turned to her, fully expecting her to join us, despite her initial protests. She had gone out and bought exercise clothes, after all. But then I saw that her face had gone three shades paler.

"Oh, Mr. David, sir," she managed to get out. "I'm not joining the class today. I'm merely an observer here to make sure my sister doesn't injure herself by doing something stupid."

David studied her for a moment. "In parkour, we don't do what is beyond our capabilities. We push ourselves, yes, but we test it first. See what our limits are. There is no room for blindly jumping into a dangerous situation. Your sister is perfectly safe here. As are you." He eyed her tracksuit. "I like the outfit."

Dottie's gaze dropped. "Thank you. Like I said, I—"

"You're worried about your knees and don't think this class is appropriate for you," he finished, eyeing the cane.

She nodded. "That about sums it up."

"Age doesn't define us," he said. "It's an excuse. Can I do the kind of stuff that Peter does with the advanced class? Yes. Can I do it as well as he does? Not anymore. It's a natural fact that our bodies regress with age. There's nothing we can do to stop it. However, there are things we can do to slow it down, and yes, even reverse the process to some extent." He pointed to her cane. "If you will give me six months, you'll be walking without that."

Dottie didn't look like she was buying what he was selling—which in this case was a weekly twenty-dollar class. But he had me caught hook, line, and sinker.

She hesitated. "I'll give you one class," she finally said. "That's all I can promise you."

David clapped his hands together, obviously pleased with her decision. "Wonderful. That's all I need."

We joined Eliza and the rest of the beginners, where we obviously belonged. Eliza began running us through a second warmup that included things like squats and lifting our knees to our chests.

This was not what I'd been hoping for, if for no other reason than when I squatted as low as Eliza encouraged us to, I couldn't get back up again. Dottie didn't even try.

I was surprised when Autumn walked up and joined the beginners. She'd said she'd been attending class since she'd returned from Paris as a way to feel a part of the community again, and she seemed plenty strong to me.

"Autumn, I really think you should join the advanced

class," Eliza said mid-squat, when our pastry chef joined the old ladies' club.

Autumn met Eliza's gaze, and I could immediately feel the tension. This was not the first time Eliza had made the suggestion.

"I've told you I'm not ready," Autumn finally said when Eliza didn't back down.

Eliza didn't answer, only shook her head and moved on with the next exercise.

"Jo," David called to me from a rock where the more advanced class was practicing jumping off, landing on the edge of a modified tire, and then rolling across the sand. The squats weren't looking so bad now. I hoped David didn't expect me to do that, even if, as he'd pointed out, I was the more adventurous one.

I smiled an apology to Eliza as I left the group, as if I had been enjoying her torturous exercises and was truly sorry I had to miss out.

"Yes, Dave?" I paused. "Can I call you that? David seems so formal." I may have even batted my eyes once or twice. It wasn't that I was romantically interested in the man—romance seemed to not be worth all the trouble it brought into someone's life, and it had never appealed to me. No, it was mostly because of the looks I was getting from the other women. Pure jealousy.

I hadn't had anyone jealous of me since...well, every Sunday when I won at bingo. But boy, did it make things more fun.

"No, you can call me David," he said, his lips pulling up at one corner.

Oh.

He continued, "I can see that we're going to need to take things slow with Dorothy, and there's nothing wrong with that. For you, though, I wanted to challenge you a bit and test to see where you're at with your balance."

I glanced up as Isaac practically dove off the large rock next to us, the sand spraying as he hit the ground just past the tire and rolled, ending up back on his feet. "I can tell you right now that I am not on this spectrum."

David laughed. "When I said that we don't fling ourselves into dangerous situations without testing the water, so to speak, I was very serious about that. Both literally and metaphorically." He pointed to a spot behind me. "We're going to start out here."

When I looked behind me, rather than seeing a tall balance beam that I was sure I wasn't yet ready for, there was a low railing that couldn't be more than six inches off the ground.

"Is that all?" I asked.

His eyes crinkled in amusement. "Hold your balance for more than five seconds by the end of class, and I'll buy you a box of Adeline's truffles."

I frowned. No longer was his smile endearing—it was mocking me. Why had he invited me over here if he thought I wouldn't even make it five seconds?

"Seconds? I'll stand on it for five minutes," I declared,

then marched over to the bar. I placed one foot on it and tested my weight on it. Seemed sturdy.

But the moment I lifted my other foot, I immediately began to fall. David was already there, and he caught me.

"You were too quick to jump on," he said. "I was going to offer you support. Let's try again, but with you cupping your hand over my fist to help you keep your balance."

I was so embarrassed that I'd fallen so quickly, even the prospect of touching Mr. Parkour did nothing for me. Heat rushed into my cheeks, and I stepped away.

"I think I'm done for today. Thank you for the lesson."

Once again, Dottie had been right. This had been a mistake. I didn't know why I'd thought I could do this.

David tried to stop me, as I'd expected he would. "No one is good at it their first day. But if you want to retain your strength and balance—if you want to remain cane-free and have the best quality of life you can—you need to practice these things. We don't become strong for the sake of being strong. We are strong to be useful. To live a good life."

Unfortunately, Dottie had heard his reference to being cane-free, even as she used her cane to help support herself as she lifted one foot, practicing her balance on the ground.

She frowned. "Is that your way of motivating people?" she asked. "Shaming them about their current condition?"

He shook his head, but his words seemed to have abandoned him. "Of course not. I was just making a point that—"

"Yes, you did make your point," Dottie said. She glanced at me. "You ready to go home?"

I was, but unfortunately, we'd ridden over with Autumn.

When I glanced over at her, she'd already stopped mid-exercise and was drinking from her water bottle, as if she'd needed the break. "Hey, I hope you two don't mind leaving class a little early, but I was thinking with such a busy evening ahead of us that I'd take you back to the bakery."

She'd recognized our dilemma and immediately come to our aid. And she didn't even make it seem like it was our fault that she was having to leave early.

"I suppose you're right," Dottie said. She nodded her goodbyes, and as we left, I called to the others, "Five-thirty tonight, I expect to see all of you at Sandcastle Bakery. It is Dottie's birthday today, and we'll be having the most amazing desserts you've had in your life, all thanks to Autumn, our resident pâtissier." I looked to Autumn. "Did I pronounce that right?"

She smiled. "Perfect."

4

"Will you run upstairs and see what's taking Dottie so long?" I asked Autumn. "People are going to be arriving any minute."

Autumn had just put the finishing touches on her French pastries, and she was admiring her handiwork. I hoped she was as impressed with them as I was—it all looked amazing. We had everything from éclairs and cheesecake to macarons and slices of the meringue cake. I'd need to make sure Autumn never caught me calling it that—for some reason it felt wrong, like an insult.

She looked to me with a grin so wide, it looked like she would burst. Autumn had always dreamed of owning her own French patisserie, and she hadn't thought it would ever happen. Certainly not in a place like Starlight Ridge.

"No need to send the girl to fetch me," Dottie's voice said from the direction of the backstairs. The old apartment above the store was the perfect space for us, but those stairs were going to kill us one of these days. They were steep and had no handrail, and just going up or down them felt no different than running a marathon.

When I turned toward the back entrance to see if Dottie needed help, Skittles took advantage of the momentary distraction. She bolted past me and leaped onto the dessert table, her front paws landing squarely on two éclairs. Both Autumn and I lunged for her before she could touch any of the other pastries. Autumn reached Skittles first, lifting her straight up, and I grabbed some napkins to wipe off her paws before we let her loose on the other side of the shop. Skittles sent us both an annoyed look before racing up toward the apartment.

"Sorry," I said, my breaths coming fast. "Sometimes I forget we have to be careful about her. She has her favorite hiding places where she sleeps most of the day, but the moment my back is turned—"

Autumn laughed. "No need to explain. I had a cat when I was a kid, and they certainly like to live life on their own terms, don't they?"

The bell over the front door rang, and I turned.

"Knock, knock," a woman said as she entered.

Florence Whitlock.

Of course she'd be the first to arrive, and early, no less.

Starlight Ridge's official church recruiter and guilt-inducer. She was likely also the gatekeeper for Heaven, from the way she threatened the rest of us with eternal damnation. Unfortunately, she was also the town's official bingo caller, a coveted position. She'd been difficult to deal with before her appointment, and impossible ever since.

The problem wasn't that Florence tried to get people to go to church or follow God's word, it was that she did it mercilessly. She'd proclaim the truths that were in the Bible and then shun you if you fell short. Like she'd done to our eldest sister, Beatrice. When Beatrice had run the souvenir shop, she'd had an entire wall filled with tarot cards and supposed healing crystals. That had certainly not gone over well with Florence, and Beatrice had been on her naughty list.

I held back a smile, because I'd reserved one of the shelves on the far wall for a picture of our sister, surrounded with crystals and a few packs of tarot cards. It wasn't gaudy or anything—just a nice memorial that fit in with the decor. In the photograph, Beatrice was holding more loaves of bread than she could possibly carry, and I thought it added a nice touch to the bakery. Autumn had supplied it—it was the only recent photo we had of Beatrice.

"Am I early?" Florence asked at the same time as her gaze landed on the memorial to Beatrice. Her smiled dipped, and she made a strangled noise. "I see you displayed some of her...items." She tried to recover gracefully, but it was painful to watch.

Even so, Florence looked beautiful, as always, her hair expertly piled on top of her head, a few stray curls framing her face. I'd never managed to get my hair to do that. She wore a tight knee-length dress and dangly earrings. I'd also never gotten away with wearing those.

"We did," I said. "She was well loved by the community, and I thought it would add a nice touch."

Florence forced a smile. "Yes, so loved." She glanced around at all the food, then back at us. "Is no one else coming?"

I glanced at the clock. She had arrived fifteen minutes early.

"They are, and they'll arrive at the appointed time," Dottie said, making an entrance. My voice caught in my throat. I didn't think I'd ever seen her looking so nice. Usually, she dressed as if she were expecting to stay inside for the rest of the day, comfort being the most important attribute to her attire.

Tonight, she was stunning and put even Florence to shame. Her blue floor-length dress shimmered as she walked, her gray hair perfectly curled, and she looked the picture of health. I was sure it was killing her—she'd opted to leave the cane hidden behind the display counter—but as more guests began to arrive, she'd never looked happier.

By the time five thirty rolled around and the party officially began, our small store didn't feel like it could hold anyone else. When Coach David, Peter, and Eliza all arrived together, I made sure to smile and wave from a safe distance. It was close enough to make them feel welcome, but not so much that we had to engage in conversation. I still felt embarrassed about how the class had gone earlier. Coach David and Eliza had both cleaned up nicely, but Peter looked like he'd come straight from class, still wearing his signature bandana and athletic clothes.

Jessie strode up to me looking for a garbage can. She'd found an empty beer bottle on the ground just outside the front door. That's all we needed—someone tripping on garbage and breaking their arm at Dottie's birthday party.

"Your bakery is beautiful," Jessie said, after tossing the bottle in the can I kept behind the counter. "It reminds me of when I was running mine. Sometimes I miss those days." She looked wistful, but then her expression turned devious. "Of course, then tourist season hits, and I'm suddenly not so nostalgic." She laughed, and I couldn't help but laugh with her.

"I think it's going to be absolutely lovely having all sorts of people to talk to," I said. "When I lived in New Mexico, I have to tell you, Jessie, I was lonely. That all changed when Dottie and I arrived here. I've never felt like I've had family and friends the way I have the past year."

I stepped back and gestured to the store. "When Dottie and I were kids, we'd never have imagined we'd be opening a bakery at our age. And yet here we are, in no small part due to you and everyone else, but certainly thanks to Autumn." I glanced around the room, looking for our pastry chef.

I spotted her on the far end talking with Florence. And she looked like she was holding back tears.

Oh, dear. That hadn't taken long.

"If you'll excuse me," I said to Jessie, then hurried over to where Florence was criticizing Autumn's éclairs as having "too much chocolate."

Florence shook her head as if she didn't know what she was going to do with Autumn. "It should accent the pastry, not take it over. Did they not teach you anything while you were in Paris?" She didn't bother keeping her voice down, and it unfortunately carried above the noise of the crowd.

How dare Florence berate the poor girl to the point she cried—I mean, over too much chocolate? There was no such thing. I pulled in a long breath so that anything I said would come out far more polite than the tongue-lashing I wanted to give the woman.

When we'd first moved to town, I'd determined to make Florence my friend. I had felt sorry for her. That had quickly dissipated over the past year. No amount of kindness and friendship had helped in the slightest. Florence Whitlock had too much anger and resentment, and she was clinging onto it like it could somehow protect her. I supposed if you repelled every kind soul who came your way, that was a protection of sorts. But I was pretty sure that wasn't what was taught in the Bible.

An idea came to me. I grabbed a stepstool from behind the counter and stood precariously on the second rung. This really should be a job for someone with better balance, as evidenced in parkour earlier that day, but I was the one who needed to do this.

"Welcome to Sandcastle Bakery," I shouted, attempting to be heard above the noise.

Despite the crowd, I was met with cheers, and I grinned. I could get used to people cheering for me, though I knew it had more to do with Autumn's food than my brilliant introduction.

"Today is Dottie's seventieth birthday," I said, "and doesn't she look lovely? Not a day over ninety."

That earned me an eye roll from Dottie and laughter from everyone else. In my defense, Dottie should have expected I'd say something like that.

"In all seriousness," I continued, "Dottie is a very special person in my life. She has always been the one to make sure I'm taken care of. We've laughed together, cried together, and run from the cops together."

That got the desired reaction, audible gasps and shocked expressions, and Dottie was quick to clarify, "She means during the annual game of flag football when I was on the police force." She shook her head, but she was also grinning, so I would take it.

"Yes, I'm sure they knew that was what I meant," I said, which was met with more laughter. "Not to take the attention away from dear Dottie, but I do want to shine the spotlight on another important woman in the room."

Erwin shouted, "Now's not the time for grandstanding, Jo. Tonight is about Dottie, not you."

I laughed, delighted. "Why thank you, Erwin, for thinking I'm important enough to make that assumption."

I waited for the laughter to die down. "No, contrary to popular belief, I am not talking about myself. Tonight is also the grand opening of Sandcastle Bakery, and none of this would have been possible without our beautifully talented pastry chef, the great pâtissier, Autumn Davis."

That sent up a cheer so loud that Autumn looked stunned, though tear tracks were still evident on her cheeks.

"As you all know, Autumn was trained in Paris but ultimately returned to our humble town and agreed to start the first French patisserie I've ever been in. I doubt you'll find another like it in all of California, and likely not the rest of the United States. She has made an assortment of delights for you to sample this evening, and if you love what you try, I will be selling whatever your heart desires so you can take it home with you." I paused. "The éclairs are especially delicious. Just the right amount of chocolate."

Autumn's lips parted in surprise, and then she smiled and mouthed, "Thank you."

"There's also a meringue cake I'm particularly fond of," I continued. "If you want to know what it's called, you'll have to ask Autumn. I can't pronounce half the things she makes, but luckily, that in no way diminishes my talent at consuming them." I held up a hand and gave a little wave. "Thank you, everyone, for coming. Stay as long as you like, and make sure to find Dottie to tell her happy birthday.

While you're at it, tell her all of the things you admire about her. I'm sure she'll love that."

No, she would hate that. Being under the spotlight and receiving compliments were two things she was allergic to, so I made sure I did both as often I as I could. I liked to think of it as a growing experience.

Adeline, our local chocolatier who owned Starlight Chocolate Confections, approached me at the counter, her plate full of every dessert we offered. "These are incredible," she said around a mouthful of food. A strawberry macaron, by the looks of it. She swallowed. "Seriously, I can't let people find out about your bakery. It will put me out of business."

I smiled. "You make gourmet truffles, something we don't have. And your store has a prominent place on the boardwalk. You're going to be fine."

She took a bite of the meringue cake, cream oozing out from the edges of the dessert, and she moaned in delight, as if to prove her point. "This dacquoise is incredible. I've had it before, but it didn't even compare to this hazelnut and strawberry. Seriously, Autumn is a magician."

Dacquoise. Dacquoise. Dacquoise.

If I said it enough times, I was bound to remember it.

"I can sell it by the slice," I said, pulling out a box. "Your wish is my command."

Adeline gave a quick nod. "Yes, please. Two slices. And two éclairs. No, make that three éclairs. And five orange macarons. I have an old college roommate coming into town for a visit, and she'd absolutely love these."

I opened the back of the display counter and pulled on a couple of disposable gloves. "If the pastries don't survive until her arrival, you know where we are. We'll be open four days a week during off season and seven days a week during tourist season."

Adeline balked. "Four days is all? How am I going to get my fix?"

I laughed. "It was a condition for Autumn to work for us, considering she's doing all the baking on her own. The poor girl needs a break sometimes, and the shorter work week is to make up for how crazy it will get in the next month or two. I suggest you stock up like a chipmunk does for winter." I paused. "Though I will say they are best fresh. Don't keep them more than a couple of days."

Adeline laughed as she handed over her credit card. "I don't think that will be a problem."

To my surprise, while Adeline and I had been talking, a line had formed. A long one.

And to my greater surprise, next in line was Florence.

"Hello, Florence. Did you get a chance to say happy birthday to Dottie?"

Florence seemed surprised by the idea and glanced behind her, where Dottie was taking a break in her chair while talking with Caleb, the scuba shop owner.

"No, not yet," Florence said stiffly, turning back. "I thought I should take care of my purchase first. Autumn likely didn't have the foresight to bake enough for this crowd, and I didn't want to risk you selling out."

Lovely. It was both an insult and a compliment to our baker.

"I'm glad you're enjoying our desserts," I said. "What can I get for you?"

Peter stepped up next to Florence at the same time I'd asked the question and said, "I need at least six eclairs. Those things were fantastic, and I need to take a few home to my mom. She was devastated she couldn't make it." His bandana had slipped and he readjusted it, his eyes eager.

Florence threw him an annoyed scowl. "Then get in line, because I was here first."

He glanced back and seemed surprised that there were, in fact, other people waiting to place their orders. "I'll be quick, I promise," he said, turning back. "I have somewhere I need to be and am in a bit of a hurry."

Florence positioned herself so her back was to Peter, like if she couldn't see him, he wasn't really there, and she eyed the various desserts in the display counter. "How many slices make up one full dacquoise cake?"

"Eight," I said, my attention split between Peter and Florence.

She gave a little nod. "Then I will have eight slices of dacquoise, please. And that will be all."

The way she said it—it was almost like she wanted to convey that the rest of the desserts weren't worthy of her attention, or her money.

But I was the face of customer service in our establishment, so I told her, "Thank you," gave her the eight dacquoise slices in our signature box, took her money, and prayed she hated the cake so much that she'd never return. It was likely the only time I'd wish for a customer to not like our food, but sometimes that extra few dollars wasn't worth it.

Or more than a few dollars. Our desserts were premium quality, after all.

Peter came to the quick conclusion that the rest of the line shared Florence's feelings about line cutting and he had to leave, though he promised he'd return the next day.

Three hours later, our bakery was empty of both people and desserts, and Dottie, Autumn, and I, slumped into a few folding chairs, surveyed the carnage.

"Happy birthday, Dottie," I said with a satisfied sigh.

Dottie beamed, taking in the empty display counter. "Did we sell out?"

Autumn nodded. "Nearly. Only a few macarons left. That means I'll need to come in early tomorrow. How much of everything should I make?"

I looked to Dottie, but she merely shrugged. "Most everyone bought stuff after trying it, so I doubt they'll be coming back tomorrow for more," she said. "Maybe aim for a third of what we sold tonight, but it doesn't have to be done by the time we open. I want you to go at whatever pace feels good to you. You've worked really hard this week, and you deserve a bit of a reprieve." She leaned back in her chair, a smile playing on her lips. "Tonight was incredible. Thank you." She tossed me a glance. "Other than the barrage of compliments, of course. Why do you always do that? You know I feel uncomfortable receiving unearned praise."

I raised my gaze to the ceiling and shook my head in disbelief. "I will continue to do it until you realize that you are an incredible human being who is deserving of nice things being said about you."

Dottie nodded slowly. "I guess I loved it, then. Couldn't get enough of people telling me what a lovely person I am. And now that I've learned my lesson, you never have to do it again."

Autumn laughed, and I joined her. It didn't matter how many years we'd spent apart, some things never changed. And my relationship with Dottie had, thankfully, been one of those things.

5

The next morning, the banging of pans in the kitchen was my alarm clock. I loved the convenience of living above the shop, but it was an old building, and I could hear everything that went on downstairs. Every movement of the mixing bowls, each murmur as Autumn talked to herself while she baked. It was comforting in some ways, but at the same time, I wouldn't have minded fifteen more minutes of sleep.

I glanced at my clock. 6:00 a.m.

Sitting up straight, I rubbed my eyes, sure I was mistaken. We didn't open until ten, and we'd told Autumn not to bother coming in until at least eight. Not after the night we'd all had.

With a little stumble in the dark, I managed to get out of bed and grab my robe.

I paused when I caught my reflection in the bathroom mirror and realized I couldn't go downstairs like this. No dignified person paraded through their place of business in their pajamas.

With a sigh, I changed into business pants and a blouse, brushed my pink locks into place, and went downstairs. The steps seemed a lot steeper at six in the morning, and I braced myself against the wall as I descended. By the time I reached Autumn, she was already preparing to inject filling into a dozen éclairs.

"What time did you get here?" I asked, still rubbing some of the sleep from my eyes.

Autumn continued with strict focus, barely acknowledging my presence. "Don't remember. Couldn't sleep."

I tilted my head to the side. "Everything okay?"

That made Autumn pause, and she glanced up. "I know it's silly, especially after selling out last night, but I couldn't stop thinking about the things Florence said to me. She asked if I had learned anything while studying in Paris, and of course I did. I know that. But my coming back here—it's not because I wasn't French like I led everyone to believe. If I would have been good enough—irreplaceable —the patisseries there would have hired me. They cared more about the desserts than my nationality." She paused and sucked in a shaky breath. "The truth is that I wasn't good enough."

I nodded in understanding and gave her a kind smile.

"And so you're here early, baking your heart out, even through all that self-doubt, because it's how you cope with stress. It's your happy place. Until someone says something unkind, and then baking also becomes your source of anxiety. Two sides of the same coin."

Autumn released a chuckle. "Yes, it is. But my éclairs have never looked better." She lifted one with a perfect shape, almost as if she had a need to prove herself to me. "The meringue for the dacquoise is just baking now. Should be done by the time I'm finished filling the éclairs. I've also been thinking that people would enjoy a Parisian flan. It's different than what people are probably used to flan being, but it's a staple in Paris, and every bakery has them. Would you be okay with my experimenting with something new?"

Autumn was spiraling now, and I walked forward and placed a hand on her shoulder.

"Hey, don't let Florence get to you. You are an amazing baker. A baker who still needs sleep. And rest. When you're finished with these, why don't you go home?"

She gave a vigorous shake of her head. "Oh, no, I don't think I can do that. There's still the macarons that need to be made and the—"

A loud knock on the front door of the shop startled us.

"That's probably Jessie, out for her morning jog," I said, willing my heart to slow.

"She always does like to keep people on their toes,"

Autumn said, smiling but looking like she'd have preferred Jessie not startle us at six-thirty in the morning.

When I walked out to reprimand her for scaring us, however, it wasn't Jessie who stood on the other side of the glass door.

I stepped back slowly and retreated into the kitchen. "It's not Jessie," I said. "It's a man. Do you think we should call the sheriff?"

I didn't even know who the sheriff was anymore. We'd just gotten a new one, but he lived in the next town over, and no one had met him yet.

"It would take him at least half an hour to get here," Autumn said, wiping her hands on her apron. "Maybe it's someone you haven't met yet or don't recognize in the dim light."

Autumn walked out into the shop but stopped by the display counter. The man was still there. He raised a hand and waved.

"I don't know him," she whispered.

The man didn't look threatening. He was clean shaven, with high cheekbones, classically handsome. Of course, many serial killers could be described as such. He wore a dark jacket, jeans, and boots. Everything nondescript.

"Can we help you?" I called, cautiously approaching the door. "We're closed and don't open for a few more hours."

The man nodded, like he understood. "I'm not here for pastries. I need to talk to an Autumn Davis."

I glanced back at Autumn, gesturing for her to stay back.

The man quirked an eyebrow, seeming confused by my reaction, but then his expression cleared. "I'm Sheriff Hart," he said. "I took up the position a few months ago. I'm sorry I haven't been out this way sooner."

I turned back to Autumn, conflicted. "What do you think I should do?" I whispered.

She hesitated. "Make him show you his badge."

When I turned back, he already had his badge out and was pressing it against the glass. It looked legitimate to me, but I also didn't know what a sheriff's badge was supposed to look like.

"What do you want with Autumn?" I asked through the glass.

The supposed sheriff released a sigh, his hands shoved in his pockets. His knees bounced, like he was cold and trying to stay warm. He glanced behind him, and that was when I noticed the sheriff's car parked in front of the shop. If he wasn't who he said he was, he'd gone to great lengths to deceive us.

"I need to talk to her about an encounter she had last night," he said, exasperation clinging to his words.

Autumn stepped forward. "You should let him in."

"Yes, I think I better." I unlocked the front door and opened it wide, ushering him in. A blast of cool air hit me, and I hurriedly shut the door. "I'm sorry. I didn't realize it was so chilly out there," I said. "And you have to understand that your sudden presence was a bit startling, considering the early hour."

Sheriff Hart seemed surprised by this revelation, and he slipped his phone out of his pocket, glancing at it. "I had no idea. I'm sorry. The sun is already up, and with something like this...well, I didn't feel like it could wait."

He fell silent, and we were all quiet for a beat longer than was comfortable. I cleared my throat.

"You mentioned that something happened last night," I finally said. "I can assure you that Autumn was with me all evening, right here in this shop. We were having a birthday party, you see. My sister. She just turned seventy. Time flies, doesn't it? It feels like we were teenagers just yesterday, arguing over borrowing each other's clothes and—"

Sheriff Hart held up his hand, stopping me mid-sentence. "Thank you, I do know that she was here in this shop. From what I understand, there was an altercation with a Ms. Florence Whitlock."

Both Autumn and I stared.

I knew that gossip traveled fast in this town, but surely it wouldn't have reached the next town over, where the sheriff lived. It wouldn't be all that interesting to them without knowing the people and the context.

"I'm surprised anyone is talking about it," I said. "Yes, Florence was rude and insulting, but that's par for the course with her. She's rude to everyone. We took care of things, so there's no need for your intervention."

Sheriff Hart had been watching Autumn, but his gaze turned on me. "That's an interesting way to phrase it. That you took care of things."

I tilted my head to the side. "Why is that interesting?"

The sheriff's gaze bore into me. "Because she's dead."

6

A utumn and I shared alarmed looks.

"What do you mean she's dead?" I asked. "If you mean she's dead set against ever returning to our bakery, you're unfortunately wrong. She bought eight slices of dacquoise last night, and what that tells me is that we have a repeat customer."

Dacquoise. I'd known if I repeated it enough, I'd finally remember. It was a bad sign if I couldn't remember the names of our most popular items.

The sheriff pursed his lips, like he thought I was purposely misunderstanding him.

I was.

There was no way that Florence was dead. She was impenetrable. She was the type of person who would always be around, always poking holes in people's happiness. She wouldn't just up and die.

"We discovered one slice of pastry in a box from your bakery on her kitchen counter," the sheriff finally said. "But we only found that to be interesting when we heard about the exchange that happened between Autumn and the deceased."

I gave Autumn a knowing look. "One slice. I told you not to listen to her. People speak their truths with their stomachs, and she loved your baking. She was just jealous she didn't have the talent herself."

Sheriff Hart was losing patience with me, his frown deepening.

"I'm sorry, Sheriff. You were wanting to ask us something, and I interrupted." I gave him the most innocent smile I could, and I had to admit, I was pretty good at it.

The sheriff shook his head and turned back to his notebook. "Autumn, do you scuba dive?"

That was an unexpected turn in the conversation.

I turned to Autumn because I was interested in the answer. I'd never scuba dived before, but I wouldn't mind learning how. Maybe we could go together sometime.

"Yes, I dive," she said slowly, as if she didn't know why he was asking and was unsure how much to say. "Everyone in town does. You grow up learning how to scuba dive and surf and swim when you live someplace like this."

That made sense. I wondered if Dottie would like to join me in learning. I'd heard that water could be good for someone's knees. It had to be better than all that dangerous parkour stuff.

"Do you own your own gear?" the sheriff asked.

Autumn nodded, though not looking like she wanted to. She nervously tucked a lock of hair behind her ear. "Like I said, it's not that unusual for around here."

I turned to Autumn. "I never knew that about you. Is it the type of thing you can easily learn in fifteen minutes, or would I need to take an actual class?"

"I believe Caleb over at the scuba shop could help you certify," the sheriff said as he scribbled a note on his pad.

My lips parted in surprise. "You know Caleb?"

Sheriff Hart glanced up. "Yes, I just met him. I stopped at his place before coming here."

I didn't like where this conversation was going, but I couldn't stop myself from asking, "And why did you stop by the scuba shop this early in the morning?"

"Because that was how Florence died. Doing a night dive. She had been stabbed and another diver found her." He glanced at his notebook. "Isaac Larson."

I lit up. "Oh, I like Isaac. He's a wonderful lifeguard, and a decent parkour ninja, from what I saw yesterday. Florence is lucky it was him who found her." I turned to Autumn. "I thought he only surfs."

She raised a shoulder, her face a couple shades paler than it had been. "Like I said, everyone here does both."

That had to have been a nasty shock. Finding someone dead in the water was one thing, but finding them dead in pitch black water—that was what nightmares were made of.

"What does any of this have to do with Autumn?" I asked. Everyone in town had had an argument with Florence at one time or another. It wasn't even gossip at this point. There had to be more to the story.

The sheriff didn't bother glancing up this time. "I have some routine questions I need to ask at the station."

Autumn folded her arms across her chest and frowned. "You can ask them here in the kitchen. It's private. But I'm not driving all the way to the next town over so you can ask me a few routine questions. That's crazy."

I could read between the lines. She was testing the sheriff. They weren't a few routine questions. He suspected her of the unthinkable. And it wasn't even her fault. Florence had been the one instigating all the drama—not Autumn.

The sheriff did look up this time, his eyebrows drawn. He remained silent, studying her.

Autumn held his gaze. "Did you have Caleb drive all the way out there when you asked him your routine questions?"

I held up a finger and looked to Autumn. "Don't say anything else, and don't go anywhere. I'll be right back."

If I could have, I would have taken the stairs two at a time. We needed Dottie. Her time on the police force should be able to help us get out of the situation.

"Dottie," I called when I finally got to the top of the stairs. I had to pause to pull in a breath, then made a beeline to her bedroom. She wasn't asleep but was still in her pajamas, sitting at her desk and writing in her journal. Skittles was curled up next to her. The panic I felt must have been obvious, and she immediately stood.

"What's wrong?"

It was such a simple question, and yet my mind went blank. Where would I even begin?

"Florence is dead," I said, "and the sheriff thinks Autumn did it because he heard about Florence berating Autumn last night, and Florence had been scuba diving at night, which I guess is a thing, and Autumn knows how to dive and owns her own equipment—"

Dottie was already out the door and saying, "That's not enough to arrest someone. I'll put a stop to it."

"Dottie, you forgot your—" I looked to her cane sitting in the corner, untouched. And Dottie hadn't had so much as a limp. In spite of the circumstances, I smiled. Maybe a little more excitement in our lives was good for Dottie. Not for Autumn, currently. But certainly Dottie. I'd need to remember that for later, once we managed to keep Autumn out of jail.

I hurried after my sister.

By the time I reached the bottom step, Dottie was in full cop mode. "Do you realize that everything you have is circumstantial? I'm not even going to give it the dignity of calling it evidence. Because it's not. Everyone in this town was at the bakery last night—it was our grand opening. Everyone has had an unpleasant encounter with Florence at some point. Everyone in this town scuba dives, and everyone owns their own equipment. You have nothing that points specifically to Autumn, and she's not going with you."

Sheriff Hart looked like he'd been caught in headlights and would rather be run over than deal with Dottie right then. "Look, Ms.—"

"My name is Dorothy, and that is all you need to know," she said, crossing her arms over her chest. "If you need to ask Autumn a few questions, fine. But she's not getting in that car with you."

The sheriff had the gall to look to me with a bewildered expression, as if I could help him. I merely smiled and lifted a shoulder. This was Dottie in her finest form.

"Like I said," he tried again, "it's just a few routine questions. According to Caleb, Florence and Autumn had an argument last night, and I can't get Florence's perspective on what happened. I'd like to at least get Autumn's."

Dottie took a menacing step toward the sheriff. "It wasn't an argument. It was an ambush. Florence Whitlock was a cruel and miserable woman, and she couldn't stand anyone else being happy. So, on what should have been one of the happiest days of Autumn's career—finally baking what she loves—she was run over by a bulldozer. And by that, I mean Florence's horrible, and untrue, words."

The sheriff held up both hands, as if in defeat. "That is why I want to talk to you," he said, turning to Autumn. "I believe it happened as Dorothy has described, but I can also imagine the kind of anger you felt after being berated like that in front of the entire town. What if they believed Florence as she was criticizing your food? Your bakery would be dead before it began." He paused. "Poor word choice."

Dottie's eyes narrowed. "I'll have you know—"

This time it was Autumn who held up a hand, having regained her composure, likely in no small part to Dottie's exuberance. "It's all right, Dorothy. I got this." She turned to the sheriff. "I wouldn't describe it as anger. It was closer to defeated. I'd worked so hard in Paris, only to be told I wasn't good enough. And now it was happening all over again. I suffer from anxiety, you see, and I struggled being able to bake with a kitchen full of people while in Paris. Even though I knew Florence was wicked and treated everyone in town like she did me, it didn't make it hurt any less. What's worse is that I stayed up half the night, her words repeating themselves in my mind over and over, and I couldn't help but start believing they were true. It made me suspect that everyone else was telling me how delicious everything was because they were just being nice and didn't want to hurt my feelings. That was my perspective. But I never hurt Florence. I'd never dream of it. I was too busy hating myself to have time to hate anyone else."

My lips parted, and I rushed forward, pulling Autumn into a tight hug. I'd known she suffered from anxiety and that baking was how she coped with it. But I hadn't realized how deep it went or how debilitating it was. "I hope I never made you feel anything even remotely close to that. Last week when I mentioned that the macarons seemed a bit on the thick side—"

Autumn gave a little laugh and pulled from my grasp. "You were absolutely right. They were." Her eyes lit up, like she'd just had an epiphany. "And I'd perfected them in time for the grand opening. Last night, they were perfect. No one could have said otherwise." She was nodding vigorously now. "And the dacquoise... It had never been more of a perfect balance between the hazelnut and the strawberries. I sampled everything myself. In the heat of the moment—all of that had disappeared, like I'd been in a fog and couldn't see past Florence and her horrible words." She looked the sheriff straight in the eye. "But last night, everything was perfect. Florence was alive the last time I saw her, and I didn't see, or speak to her, after she left. That is all that you need to know."

The sheriff gave a hesitant nod, like he hadn't expected to be ambushed by three ladies in a bakery this early in the morning and he was uncertain how to proceed.

"Thank you for your statement," he finally said. "I'd appreciate contact information for the three of you, just in case I have further questions."

I walked over to the display counter and picked up a business card. "You can reach any of us here, during business hours. We'd be happy to take your call."

Sheriff Hart took the card from my outstretched

fingers. "A landline? I didn't know anyone had one of those anymore."

I gave a quick nod. "Yes. A landline. There are some people I prefer not have full access to my time." I gave him a pointed look to ensure he knew that he was one of those people.

From his surprised expression, it had done its job. "I see," he said, closing his notepad and slipping it back into his pocket. "I'll call if I have any further questions, then. During business hours." His gaze swept the room, ultimately landing on the front door, the sky already bright, despite the early hour. "Seems like I'll be spending a lot of time in your little town over the next while. What's the best place to grab breakfast?"

Dottie took this one. "Follow the road that leads out of town—" Sheriff Hart immediately frowned, and she held up a hand. "Let me finish. If you walk ten minutes up the road, there is a little diner on the right-hand side. Jo likes their biscuits and gravy, but I prefer the pancakes."

"I'm a breakfast burrito girl, myself," Autumn said, seeming to have recovered from this morning's interrogation—or lack thereof.

Sheriff Hart gave the three of us one last long look, then a little nod. "I appreciate the recommendation. Thank you."

We watched through the large front windows as he drove away and the town began to awaken and come to life.

"Do you think that's the last we've seen of him?" Autumn finally asked.

I shook my head. "Unfortunately, no. It seems to me that the sheriff is currently without suspects. And without real evidence, he's grasping at straws. I believe you are that straw, my dear. But don't worry, we won't let him do anything to you. You are under the protection of the Darby sisters."

Autumn's lips quirked up at the edges. "I like the sound of that. It makes you sound like your own special version of the mafia, except that I don't have to buy your protection."

I laughed. "That's cute that you think that. But if I'm not mistaken, you pay us with delicious pastries."

Autumn's eyes widened. "The meringue. I left it in the oven." And then she ran into the kitchen, leaving Dottie and me alone.

"He'll be back," Dottie said, her voice soft.

"I know."

"And if he finds evidence that could implicate Autumn further, we can't stop him from taking her to the station."

I paused. "I know that too." I glanced at Dottie. "She didn't do it, though."

Dottie hesitated. "Autumn is a sweet girl. But she has so much anxiety bottled up in that mind of hers. Stuff like that—it can make a person snap. When the world is too much and it seems like there is no way out, a normally wonderfully good person can do terrible things. I saw it all the time when I was on the force. And they were always the hardest cases to work."

I held her gaze. "She didn't do it. And if it's up to us to prove it, we will."

Dottie gave a small nod. When she turned to leave, I called to her, "Oh, by the way, you forgot your cane. And you never even noticed."

7

E ven though Autumn had said she was fine and that she wanted to work as usual, she most definitely wasn't fine. Every time I popped my head in to check on her, she jumped like she was about to be attacked. She'd smile and laugh, telling me I had startled her. But I saw the fear in her eyes.

Autumn was terrified that any minute the sheriff was going to return and she'd have no choice but to leave with him. And then there was the worst fear—the fear of not returning.

I'd doubted we'd sell much today and begged her to take the rest of the day off. But as soon as I flicked on the OPEN sign, we had customer after customer. As grateful as I was for the instant success of our little bakery, I worried what it would look like once things really got going in the next month or two.

This gave Autumn no choice but to continue working.

"I'm going to help you," I said, pulling on an apron. "It's not fair that you shoulder the burden of baking everything on your own. Dottie can handle the cash register."

Autumn looked at me like I had lost my mind. "You don't just pick up a whisk and suddenly know how to make éclairs." When I didn't make a move to leave, she released a sigh. "Look, I know that you're worried about me, but I need to be alone back here. It's the way I work. I never did like relying on someone else, even another chef, and I'm sure Dottie could use your help out there."

I didn't like the thought of leaving Autumn alone, but if that was what she needed, I'd give it to her.

It was around lunchtime when I went back to see if she had any more orange macarons since we'd sold out. I couldn't believe how many repeat customers we'd had from the previous evening. I'd known that Autumn was good—I'd eaten plenty of her pastries over the past few months—but the response from the community was exceeding my wildest expectations.

"Autumn, do you by any chance have—" I stopped mid-step. Autumn wasn't there. She was probably taking a bathroom break, so I looked in the industrial-size fridge for any macarons that might already be finished. Several display trays sat on the shelves, and they were filled with a variety of pastries, including orange macarons, all ready to be taken to the front.

When I reached for the tray of macarons, I heard the

whistling of wind and glanced toward the back door. It was cracked open. Could be nothing. Autumn sometimes opened it to let some fresh air in.

Except, on my way back up to the front with the macarons, I noticed the bathroom door wide open.

Autumn wasn't here.

She'd left, which was what I'd been trying to get her to do all morning, but the way she'd sneaked out the back door—something was wrong. She knew she could have told us if she needed to go home for the rest of the day. We'd have understood, and when we'd sold out of what we had up front, we'd have closed up. It wasn't a big deal to us. That was one of the nice things about retirement— you did what you wanted and told everyone else to deal with it.

I took the tray of orange macarons to the display counter.

"We also need éclairs, dacquoise, and madeleines," Dottie said, tossing me a glance as she helped Mr. Mueller with his purchase. This time of year was slow for most of the town, and it seemed that included the local market, which Mr. Mueller and his wife owned.

"I can't get enough of the madeleines," he said. "The lime that's in there, it's something else."

I gave him a smile. "Thank you so much. I'll be sure to pass the compliment on to Autumn." I waited until he left to talk to Dottie. "We have a couple trays of éclairs and dacquoise in the back, but that is all we have for the rest of the day. Autumn is gone, and I have no idea where. Snuck out the back."

Dottie frowned. "That's very unlike her."

"Is it so unusual for someone who has been accused of murder, though?" I asked.

"She hasn't been accused. It makes sense that the sheriff would want to ask her questions." Dottie said it with such conviction, I almost believed her.

Almost.

"You know that Autumn has extreme anxiety, and I think it's what led to her not being hired in the patisseries in France. Despite what she says, she's obviously good enough, but she has this need to work alone. I doubt that was something they could accommodate there. She's finally found the perfect situation for herself, and now a woman ends up murdered, with the sheriff looking at Autumn as a suspect. Of course her anxiety is going to kick in—she's at risk of losing everything."

Dottie remained quiet for a moment. "You know who else runs when the cops get too close?"

My gaze hardened. "I told you that Autumn isn't guilty."

Dottie gave a little nod, but I could tell she wasn't entirely convinced. She'd seen too much in her career to dismiss Autumn being a murderer as a plausible scenario.

"Fine. You want proof? I'm going to find you proof." I grabbed my jacket off the back counter and stormed toward the front door. I glanced back just long enough to say, "The éclairs and dacquoise are in the fridge, all ready to go."

And then I finished storming out, choosing a direction and going with it, because I didn't want to lose momentum until Dottie could no longer see me.

I PULLED IN A LONG BREATH, relishing the salty air as I made my way toward the boardwalk. The sea air had done more good for me than I could have ever dreamed, and I could now walk most anywhere I wanted without getting winded. When I'd first moved to Starlight Ridge, I'd sold my car, knowing that Dottie had one if I ever needed it, but I hadn't asked for a ride in months.

Caleb was just opening his scuba shop, and he waved me over.

"Need to make another order?" I teased.

He gave me a smile that said he was humoring me and said, "No, I think last night's order should last me at least the day. I'll probably be back tomorrow, though." Caleb then paused, as if he had something else on his mind and he was trying to find the words. "The sheriff visited me early this morning—said it couldn't wait."

I gave a knowing nod. "Yes. Poor Florence. I may have had my troubles with the woman, but she deserved better than this. Killed while scuba diving, is that right?"

"A knife of some kind," he said. "The sheriff wanted to know if I sold any, which he had to have already known.

Any diver, especially one who enjoys night diving, has a knife on them."

I eyed the peaceful water warily, suddenly imagining all the sea monsters that must live under the unassuming waves. "Why? Do you get attacked that often?"

Caleb tilted his head to the side, like he'd assumed I knew something about diving. "No, but you could easily get snagged on kelp or netting and need to cut it away. It can also be used as a tool or for fishing—there's a million different reasons you'd want to dive with one."

"Other than murder," I helpfully added.

He gave me a long look. "Yes, other than murder."

"I suppose the sheriff knows that, if he grew up around the ocean," I said thoughtfully. "He won't think you actually did it, though he might come around a lot more now that he thinks you inadvertently provided the murder weapon."

Caleb gave a start. "What do you mean by that?"

"Did he ask to see your personal knife?" I asked.

He nodded.

"And did he take it with him?"

Caleb eyed me as if he wasn't sure what to make of the question. "No, he didn't. I suppose he was satisfied that I had nothing to do with it." He looked a bit antsy, his mind no doubt jumping to the alternative scenario. "Look, I was just trying to give you fair warning because I think I made too big a deal about the argument between Autumn and

Florence at the party. I didn't mean to make trouble for Autumn."

I waved a hand through the air. "Yes, yes, I know. But tell me more about these knives you sell. Did Autumn own one?"

Caleb released a long sigh. "I'm telling you that every person in this town owns one of these knives. It could have been anyone. We all dive, and we all know the safety precautions we should take."

Everyone dove with a knife.

Including Florence.

I rummaged in my pocket and pulled out the sheriff's card. "Would you be so kind as to let me use your phone?" I asked Caleb. "It's important."

It was an abrupt change of conversation, and Caleb didn't seem to know what to think of it, but he ultimately agreed and slipped his phone out of his pocket.

The sheriff's phone rang only once before he answered, "Sheriff Hart." He sounded a bit annoyed at being interrupted from whatever he'd been doing.

"Sheriff, it's Jo. From the bakery. You know, the one you arrived at unannounced this morning and scared me and my pastry chef half to death."

The sheriff, who had previously sounded like he could do without my call, now sounded quite alert. "What do you have, Jo? I could use some good news."

He hadn't found anything useful. That was good news for Autumn. Or maybe it was bad.

"Was Florence wearing a diving knife when you found her?" I asked, getting to the point.

A hesitation. "No. Why?"

"Because I understand that you are harassing poor Caleb at his dive shop. That isn't going to do you any good, because no one in their right mind would use their own knife. Why do that when everyone in town owns one? You would use someone else's."

The sheriff was quiet for a moment. "You're saying the killer used Florence's knife."

"Yes, sir. No self-respecting diver would go night diving without their knife, everyone knows that. I suspect you will find Florence's knife at the bottom of the ocean, though. That's a tough break, and I wish you all the best retrieving that."

Before the sheriff could ask any questions I didn't know the answer to, I hung up. I needed to keep the upper hand on this thing.

I handed Caleb back his phone. "There. You shouldn't have any additional trouble from the sheriff about your knives."

The dive shop owner was staring at me, his lips parted.

"You're going to catch flies, dear," I said, then turned away, wondering where my next stop should be.

"How did you figure out that the killer used Florence's own knife?" Caleb asked.

I turned slightly. "Logic, mostly. It's quite useful for things like murder investigations, though it's not going to help me find Autumn. I haven't the foggiest idea where she'd be. Did you by any chance see her in the past hour?"

He shook his head. "Sorry, I didn't."

"It's all right. I didn't think you would have. I don't think she wants to be seen at the moment."

And then I turned my attention to the situation at hand. Florence had been killed with her own knife while diving. Everyone in town knew how to dive. That wasn't much to go on. The sheriff no doubt was stuck on Autumn because of her argument with Florence, as well as Caleb because he owned the dive shop.

I turned back to where Caleb was placing his OPEN sign in the window. "Who do you think did it? Killed Florence, I mean. I'm wondering if I should start locking my front door at night. This seemingly quiet town has had two murders in the past year."

Caleb smiled. "Oh, you don't need to worry about that. Florence—she seemed to bring out the worst in people, and you don't have that problem. If you ask me, it was probably someone in the church. They're all about destroying the wicked, aren't they?" He then turned and disappeared inside his shop.

8

That was an interesting idea, and one that didn't sit well with me. It wasn't that I thought the folks at church weren't capable of something like this—taking out Florence in the name of religion. They absolutely were. But considering all the times the pastor had taught mercy, forgiveness, and turning the other cheek, I'd hoped they were better than that.

Of course, taking things to the extreme like Florence tended to do, who knew what to expect from that lot.

I was a regular churchgoer, so I knew all the usual ladies. My attendance wasn't because I felt particularly drawn to the concept of religion—now that I was older, it seemed that it provided more doom and gloom than when I'd been a child. Maybe it had something to do with me constantly being told that I had limited time until I met my Maker, that I'd better make sure I had all my ducks in a row and my repentance all squared away, and that I shouldn't be displaying the tarot cards and crystals that my late sister had sold in her souvenir shop.

No, it certainly had nothing to do with religion. I continued to attend because right after church on Sunday was bingo, and if you attended services, you received an extra card.

My bingo prizes tended to outweigh the guilt-inducing sermons, so every Sunday at 10:00 a.m., Dottie, Autumn, and I attended together.

The only problem was that today was Saturday and I couldn't wait until tomorrow to question the ladies at church. Even one day could make a huge difference for Autumn. That meant I'd need to figure out the old-fashioned way who at church had a vendetta against Florence.

Gossip.

With all this excitement, though, there was something I needed to take care of first. A nap. I'd never make it through the day without it.

"WHERE HAVE YOU BEEN?" Dottie demanded the moment I stepped into the bakery. "This place has been packed, and I've had a difficult time explaining to people that I need to close early because I no longer have a baker or business partner."

I slipped my jacket off and placed it behind the counter. "I told you I'm going to prove Autumn is innocent, with or without your help. I'm sorry we've needed to close early, but if we don't find who killed Florence, we may be closing permanently." I turned toward the stairs that led toward the apartment but paused to glance back at Dottie. "I could use your help. You think Autumn could have done it, that's the cop in you, but I'm not willing to make that assumption."

That gave Dottie pause, and after a moment of consideration, she gave a small nod. "Okay. What do you need?"

"A nap. And food. I'm starving."

"The diner it is."

I had planned on just making myself a sandwich, but now that Dottie had mentioned the diner, I was suddenly craving Lars' fish tacos and french fries. It took me less than thirty seconds to turn around, grab my jacket, and head back out the front door. Dottie locked up behind me and started toward her car.

We always drove because of Dottie's knees, but I'd seen her that morning do just fine without her cane. She leaned on it now as she opened the car door, but I had a feeling it was more out of habit than anything. She'd gotten stronger, she just wouldn't admit it.

"Where are you going?" I asked, not moving toward the car. "It's a beautiful day. Let's walk."

Dottie stared. "You know I would never make it."

I pointed to the cane. "You didn't need it at all this morning when you thundered down the stairs to give Sheriff Hart a piece of your mind, and even now, you're not leaning on it as much as you used to. Come on, give it a try."

Dottie hesitated, as if the cane was more than just a tool. It was security.

"All right," she finally agreed. "But if I don't make it, you're the one who has to walk back and retrieve the car."

I was shocked she'd agreed to walk, but I wasn't one to give her the chance to change her mind, so I immediately began the ten-minute journey to the outskirts of town.

Dottie walked slower than I thought necessary, as if she were proving a point, and I paused to allow her to catch up. She could walk as slowly as she wanted, but I wasn't going to give in and go back for the car.

We were halfway to the diner when I saw Isaac approaching from the other direction, a burger in hand. He wasn't your typical Californian blond surfer. Instead, he had a dark complexion and even darker hair. All the women in town went crazy for him, and the tourists were even worse. He never seemed to notice, though. All he cared about was surfing, and anything else that could get him closer to the ocean.

"Morning, Isaac," I said. "How are the waves treating you?"

Even though I asked him the same question every time we met, it struck a different chord today. Because yesterday, the waves had brought him a dead body. I winced.

If he'd noticed the poor choice of words, he didn't let on, instead giving me his signature easygoing smile. He stopped walking, as did Dottie and I. "Didn't go out this morning, unfortunately. Had some stuff to do. But tomorrow we're supposed to have better waves anyway."

Stuff to do. Like being questioned by the sheriff about a murder.

I hesitated, wondering if it would be okay for me to press him for more information. Then I remembered that people thought I was old, which meant I could get away with a lot more.

"I can't imagine the shock you must have felt when you discovered Florence," I told him, giving him my most sympathetic eyes. "I mean, honestly, if that had been me, I wouldn't ever be able to go back in the water. No one should have to go through something like that." I rested a hand on his arm. "Are you doing okay?"

That had been too much, even from me, and I immediately saw his defenses rise. He saw me as he did everyone else—someone looking for the latest gossip. Which was true, but not for the reasons he was thinking. Most people in town merely wanted gossip to entertain themselves—something to do to pass the time while they waited for tourist season to kick in.

What he didn't realize was that I wasn't asking for my own benefit.

"I'm fine," he mumbled. "Thank you for asking."

Always the gentleman.

Dottie looked at me with a warning in her eyes, letting me know I had to let it go and move on. But maybe if Isaac knew the reason this was important to me, he would be more understanding.

"We're worried about Autumn," I said, my voice quiet. "Sheriff Hart has taken a special interest in her. That's crazy, of course—she isn't capable of anything like that—but all the same, I really wish he'd focus his attention on someone else."

As soon as I said it, I realized I didn't want anyone in our small town to be capable of hurting someone the way they had Florence. Who would I choose to put in Autumn's place?

No one.

Isaac's gaze snapped to me. "Why would he suspect Autumn? It can't be because of the incident at your bakery last night. That was nothing compared to what Florence did to Clarissa Johnson last week."

Clarissa Johnson. I only knew her by sight. She was in her mid-forties and always sat in the second row at church and kept to herself. Kind of a homely woman. Had a son that still lived in town, but no husband that I was aware of.

"What did Florence do to Clarissa?" Dottie asked, her interest now piqued.

Isaac hesitated. "I'm not one to gossip."

"Well, of course not," I said. "None of us are."

That seemed to be enough for him, and he jumped into his story without any further hesitation. "Last week, you two missed bingo or you would have witnessed it first hand."

"Stupid head cold," I muttered. "I wanted to go, but Dottie said we'd infect the whole town if we so much as left our beds. I bet everyone was winning right and left without me there. Well, they shouldn't get used to it, because tomorrow, I'm cleaning out the place." That was when I remembered that Florence was the official bingo caller. "Oh dear, they're probably going to have to cancel until they can get a new caller, aren't they?"

Dottie and Isaac stared at me.

"But this isn't about me," I said, suddenly self-conscious. "Continue."

Isaac's lips pulled up at the corners. "Florence had only been our bingo caller for a few months, but you know how insufferable she could be. You couldn't talk with her more than a few seconds without her bringing it up, like it was the best thing that had ever happened to her, or to anyone else, for that matter."

It was true. I had seen it first hand, and if I'd thought people had avoided spending time with her before, it had only gotten worse. It was like she had gone out of her way to alienate herself.

"Let me guess, she used the gavel," Dottie said. "And then got mad at Clarissa for daring to whisper during a game because she might not hear the next number that was called. Heaven forbid we have any fun while playing." She turned to me. "Have you noticed that church attendance has gone down since Florence became the official bingo caller?"

I nodded. "No one cares about the extra card anymore, which is a shame. Pastor Rick tries so hard, and yet we all have to be bribed to be there."

"That's not what happened," Isaac said. He was smiling, but his voice was full of exasperation.

Dottie was the one who apologized this time, then waved a hand through the air. "Please, continue."

Isaac pulled in a long breath, as if bracing himself for another interruption. When none came, he pressed on. "Florence was calling out the numbers as usual, but she was just getting over a cold, and people couldn't hear in the back."

I nudged Dottie. "See, even she didn't let a little cold stop her. Though she's probably where we got ours."

Isaac eyed me before continuing. "As quiet as Clarissa is, it turns out that she has some strong lungs. She started repeating the numbers from where she sat at the front table so everyone could hear, and it got to the point where she sounded like a myna bird. Ultimately, Clarissa ended up picking up her cards, set herself up at the front of the room next to Florence, and started calling the numbers out as soon as Florence picked up the ball, filling out her own card as she did so."

I grimaced and turned to Dottie. "The one week we're gone, and that's when all the excitement happens. We're never missing bingo again. Even for a cold."

"Florence went ballistic, I'm sure," Dottie said, ignoring me. "Autumn told me she's coveted that bingo position for years. And now that it was finally hers, it was being yanked right out from under her."

It was Isaac's turn to grimace. "Ballistic is a good way to put it. Florence went off on Clarissa in ways that had nothing to do with bingo. Personal attacks about Clarissa's failed relationships, the lack of achievements in her life, and that being the reason Clarissa was trying to steal Florence's. It got really nasty."

As bad as I felt for Clarissa, I felt equally sad for Florence. The past year I'd known her, she'd been so unhappy that she'd clung to anything that gave her life meaning. But that desire for a meaningful life was what had led her to drive people away. Initially, I'd hoped I could break through her hard shell and we'd become friends. Or at the very least, friendly acquaintances. But Florence had seemed determined to be alone, and she'd hurt many people in the process.

"That sounds about right. Her interaction with Autumn last night went about the same," Dottie said with a small nod.

"But did Autumn pick up the bingo ball cage and throw it across the room and threaten to kill Florence if she dared ever show up to bingo again? Clarissa claimed that I-19 hadn't been called in three weeks and that Florence had been tampering with the bingo balls to keep certain people from winning. It only got worse from there."

I tried to keep a neutral, listening smile. But inside, my heart had dropped, and my palms grew clammy.

Unfortunately, I knew where I-19 had ended up.

I had meant to return the ball the next week but had forgotten. Same with the week after that.

Dottie glanced at me. She also knew where I-19 had ended up.

I'd been able to hide my kleptomania from my sister for years, but the lies had started adding up, as had the number of earrings that made the journey from her bedroom into mine.

I'd visited a therapist for a while, but it hadn't done much good.

And now look what it had led to.

The way Isaac had described the bingo situation—it didn't sound like the Clarissa I'd seen in the second pew of church each Sunday. Dottie had said that even good people could be pushed past their breaking point and do terrible things—maybe Clarissa was one of those people.

And it had been I-19 that had pushed her over the edge.

This was all my fault. If I'd had one ounce of self-control and not added the stupid ball to my stash of pens and other odd items I'd swiped over the years, and just put it back like I'd intended, Florence might still be alive.

I sucked in a long breath and let it out slowly, focusing on what my doctor had told me. It was a medical condition. It had nothing to do with self-control.

"Biological" was the word he'd used while glancing at my mother.

"No," I finally said, breaking the silence that had settled over us. "Autumn did not react in the same way." I paused. "Does Sheriff Hart know what happened at bingo?"

Isaac lifted a shoulder. "I have no idea. Honestly, last night I was in a state of shock and could barely answer the sheriff's questions." He released a humorless laugh. "I almost thought he suspected me for a little bit. No one else was around when I found Florence on the beach."

I tilted my head. "You didn't find her in the water?"

"Nope. She must have been just about to go in, because she was completely dry."

I supposed the diving knife could still be at the bottom of the ocean, if someone had a good throwing arm and could get it far enough out there.

"There is something else," he said slowly. "I mentioned it to the sheriff, but he didn't seem to think it was important. Two empty beer bottles were next to her on the beach."

That gave Dottie pause. "How did you know they were empty?"

"I tripped on one when approaching her. Couldn't see them in the dark." He studied us, as if expecting a bigger reaction. When it was apparent that we had no idea why this was important, he explained. "Everyone who dives knows you shouldn't drink alcohol before going out in the water, especially on a night dive. Not only does it impair your judgment, but it can increase the risk of nitrogen narcosis. If she was going to dive while drunk..."

His voice trailed off.

"What would that mean?" I asked, my voice quiet.

Isaac hesitated. "She was trying to escape something. Emotionally. Nitrogen narcosis is caused by the anesthetic effect of certain gases at high pressure. Meaning, the deeper you go, the more pressure, the greater the effects. The most benign symptoms are things like a feeling of tranquility—a mastery of your environment. It actually feels really amazing. Like you're on top of the world. If you recognize what's happening and return to shallower water, it's not a big deal. But if you go deeper, you start losing your cognitive functions. You can have trouble making decisions, get vertigo, and even paranoia."

"Do you think... Florence wasn't trying to kill herself, was she?" I asked.

I suddenly realized that I didn't know where on her body she had been stabbed. If it had been her own knife, had she been the one to do it?

Dottie met my gaze. We'd known Florence was a troubled woman, but maybe we hadn't realized just how troubled.

9

"I'm not feeling so hungry anymore," I said to Dottie as we watched Isaac disappear down the road. "I'd been looking for gossip, but that wasn't idle chitchat. That was some really heavy stuff." I turned to her. "Do you think if I wouldn't have stolen that bingo ball—"

Dottie was already shaking her head. "None of this is your fault, Jo. No one dies over bingo. And before you go down that other road, Florence didn't off herself. Even if she did, it shouldn't get between us and our lunch." And then she swung her cane with a dramatic flair before leaning on it and continuing up the road.

I hurried to catch up with her. "Sometimes I forget that you've seen some pretty horrific things. Are you ever troubled at the level of desensitization you've achieved?"

Dottie glanced at me. "No. Why, should I be?"

"Yes."

"Why?" she asked again.

That was a legitimate question, and I was having trouble coming up with a legitimate answer.

She released a tired sigh. It seemed this walk was taking more out of her than I'd anticipated. Or maybe she was just tired of having to deal with me twenty-four hours a day. After not seeing each other for seven years, it was so good to be back in each other's lives. But we'd gone from near-zero interaction to living together, and I didn't think we'd been prepared for the shock of it all.

"When you're a cop, you have to compartmentalize," she said, not looking at me as we walked. "It protects you from all the awfulness. Those separate compartments are required to be able to do your job. It's not troubling to me —it's survival. I can keep a level head in a situation that would have most people running for the hills. Society needs people like me, and I was always happy to carry the burden. Because I knew it mattered. It was important. It still is."

I'd never thought about it like that, and my sister had never opened up about that part of her life to me before. "Thank you for telling me, Dottie. And thank you for your service."

She laughed at that. "You're welcome."

We were nearly to the diner when I asked, "Why don't you think she killed herself?"

Dottie stopped for a moment, resting on her cane. "Because she would never give Clarissa, or anyone else for that matter, the satisfaction. Florence prided herself on being better than everyone else, and she'd received the town's most coveted position—the official bingo caller. She wasn't going to give that up just because Clarissa upstaged her. No, Florence was the type who would merely come back better, and stronger. More visible. More likely than not, she'd show that strength through revenge."

It was terrifying to hear what went on in Dottie's mind sometimes. I couldn't imagine what it was like for her having to live with those thoughts, day in and day out.

"By the same token," I said, "I haven't heard a single motive that I think is strong enough for something like murder. No one is going to kill her because they want to be the bingo caller, and even though she was a terrible and callous human being, was that really enough? There are plenty of those people in the world, and we've learned to live with them. There has to be more to it than that."

Dottie began walking again. "You'd be surprised what people will kill for. Road rage is a real thing, and it doesn't just happen while driving. We all have a certain pride within us, and when we feel disrespected, sometimes our emotions get the best of us. Florence never made it into the water, which means she must have had an encounter on the beach. Someone had reached their breaking point. They'd had enough."

We reached the diner, and I held the door open for Dottie. "I suppose. It's just hard to imagine."

Dottie tossed me a smile as we approached the counter. "That's because you're the happiest, kindest person on the planet." She eyed my hair. Today it had blue streaks. "Your goal in life is to make everyone's lives better. That's a gift that not everyone has. Even your hair makes my day better." I smiled and was about to thank her for the compliment when she added, "Of course, it's mostly because it makes me laugh that I never know what color your hair is going to be when I wake up in the morning, and I doubt you remember either. Not until you look in the mirror, that is."

I was unsure if that was a compliment, but I was still going to take it as one.

"Thank you," I said, then turned to Lars, who was patiently waiting behind the counter for us to finish our exchange.

Lars was not the type of person you expected to be running a diner in the outskirts of a small seaside town. He was a large man, tattoos covering his arms, and bald. He looked more like he should be a bouncer at an exclusive club.

"Hey, Lars, what's the special today?" I asked, shooting him a large smile. He returned it, which I had been counting on. He had the best smile—the kind that crinkled the corners of his eyes.

"Enchilada plate," he said. He threw a glance toward Dottie. "Not for you, though. I'll make an exception and give you a discount on the bean and cheese burrito plate."

"It was one time," Dottie protested. "I can handle spicy, I swear."

Lars laughed and shook his head. "No, you can't. Last time, I thought I was going to have to call for the paramedics."

"It was one time," Dottie grumbled, but then pointed to the left side of the menu. "Fine. I'll get your soup and salad. Cheddar broccoli soup, please. That way you won't have to resuscitate me." She said it like she was trying to make a jab at Lars, but he merely gave a satisfied nod.

"Thank you." He turned to me. "And you?"

"I'll go for the enchilada plate." I tried not to look at Dottie. She'd think I was ordering it to rub it in that I could handle spicy. I'd lived in New Mexico for two decades, so there wasn't anything Lars could give me that would faze me. However, Dottie had nothing to do with my decision. I wanted Mexican food, and it just so happened to be on special. "And a cup of water. Because I'm thirsty, not because it's spicy."

That one had been for Dottie's benefit.

Lars chuckled. "Thanks for clarifying." He turned to grab a couple of cups for us. "Isaac was just in here. Sounds like some crazy stuff happening over in town, which would explain why it's been such a slow morning.

One of the reasons I'm happy to be a little away from it all. Never liked the drama."

Sure, I guess it could be called that.

"Did you know her?" I asked, taking my cup from him.

Lars leaned on the counter. "Florence? Naw. She never came out here. Too good for my food, I guess. But I knew plenty about her. Everyone had something to say, and it made me glad that I didn't have the pleasure of making her acquaintance. Sounded like a real piece of work. Just the other day, Clarissa Johnson came in, fuming. Said that one day Florence was going to get what was coming to her and Clarissa hoped it was sooner than later. Something about bingo over at the community center." He paused. "What is with you people and bingo? The guy calls out a number, you place a token on the number. That's it. And yet everyone goes crazy over it."

I tried to not take it personally. I knew he didn't mean anything by it, he just hadn't had the opportunity to experience it for himself. "Think of it more like gambling," I said. "Really, we're all just there for the prizes."

Lars' eyes lit up in understanding. "Okay, so it's a game of luck, and you're there for the thrill when you hit the jackpot. I guess I can see how that could be fun."

I held up a finger. "I never said it was a game of luck. No, there's real skill involved. I'm quite good at it myself. Always take home the best prizes."

He tilted his head, confused. "But you just said it was

like gambling. And that's worse than a game of luck. At a casino, there is a statistical probability that you'll lose."

I could see the conversation had gotten away from me. "It doesn't matter. The point is that Florence was the official bingo caller, and that's a coveted position in this town. They have to be appointed by town council and everything."

Lars grunted. "Don't I know it. I was hearing about it for weeks after Florence was appointed. People weren't happy that she'd been chosen, and they all assumed it was because the town council didn't want any trouble. Figured it would be easier just to give it to her than deal with the fallout if they gave it to someone else. I can understand how that wouldn't sit right with folks around here, considering their feelings toward the woman. If you ask me, they're still blaming her for the death of Clarissa's boy. I was surprised that Florence stayed in Starlight Ridge after all that."

Dottie and I exchanged alarmed looks.

"What do you mean?" I asked.

Lars gave us a quizzical look. "You've lived here an entire year and you don't know?" He gave a sad shake of his head. "The way I heard it, Florence and Clarissa used to be friends. There was one day when Clarissa had an appointment in the city and asked Florence to watch her younger son for a few hours while she was away. The boy was probably only about six or seven. He wandered outside because he wanted to play in the ocean. Florence didn't notice until it was too late. He'd drowned."

My hand flew to my mouth. "That's awful."

Dottie looked like she might be sick and turned away.

"Clarissa hasn't been the same since," Lars said. "Neither has her other son—he took it especially hard. It tore that family apart."

"You sure she didn't kill herself?" I murmured to Dottie. "If I were living with that kind of guilt, it would be very tempting."

The door to the diner opened, and Jessie and Adeline walked in.

"Jo and Dorothy," Jessie said, walking over and giving us big hugs. "I heard your shop is closed for the rest of the day. I hope this has nothing to do with that nasty Florence business. You shouldn't allow that woman to affect even one more day of your life. She gave you enough trouble as it was."

Dottie raised an eyebrow. "You're saying we shouldn't allow a woman being murdered to affect us? She might not have been our favorite person in the world, but she still didn't deserve what happened to her."

"Well, of course not," Jessie said, looking offended that we'd assumed that was what she'd meant. "But Sheriff Hart has things covered on his end, doesn't he? Meanwhile, the rest of us are left to suffer. I was looking forward to some macarons. Adeline said both the orange and strawberry are equally good, but I haven't had the chance to test that theory myself."

"What about the truffles from my shop?" Adeline protested. "You've certainly been eating plenty of those the last few days, so I wouldn't say you've been suffering."

Jessie laughed. "Yes, and your truffles are amazing. But one can't live on chocolate alone, and you've tried Autumn's macarons."

Adeline conceded, "It's true, they really are delicious."

Dottie and I exchanged looks, like we didn't know how much we should say about the situation with Autumn, but Jessie immediately noticed. "What's happened?"

"We may not be baking any macarons for a few days. We don't know where Autumn is," I said, my words slow. "The sheriff stopped by to question her about her exchange with Florence, and it freaked her out."

Jessie snorted. "Exchange. More like attack."

"Exactly," Dottie said. "That's how everyone else has explained it to the sheriff too, and then Florence ends up dead. You can see how that looks."

Adeline's eyes widened. "You're saying that he thinks Autumn actually did it?" She shook her head. "She helped me out in my chocolate shop a few summers back, and that woman doesn't have a killer's spirit."

I raised my hands in a defensive gesture. "You're preaching to the choir."

Jessie nodded slowly. "I may know where she is, and if

I'm correct, then she's safe." She paused. "I'm not sure I should say anything, though. Just in case."

"Just in case of what?" I asked.

She hesitated. "Well, let's just say Dorothy is a former cop, right?"

Dottie turned to me, realization in her gaze. "Autumn thinks I'll turn her over to Sheriff Hart. She's not running from just him. She's running from us too."

10

Not only did Autumn think that Dottie would turn her over to the sheriff, if it came down to it, but apparently Jessie did too. There was no other reason she wouldn't be willing to share Autumn's location.

After placing our orders, Dottie and I found a booth on the opposite side of the diner from Jessie and Adeline. It wasn't that we didn't want to eat with them, but the things that Dottie and I had to discuss would be better in private.

As much as I loved Jessie and appreciated everything she did for our town, she knew everything about everyone. It was mostly because she cared so much, but she had no problem spreading it when the mood suited her.

Which it apparently hadn't, when it came to Autumn's location. That was another attribute of Jessie's—loyal to a fault.

I took a bite of my enchilada and then glanced up at

Dottie. "We need to help Autumn. As a cop, you hated when people interfered with your investigations. It made it harder to do your job. I get that. But don't you think we could make an exception here?"

Dottie chewed far longer than necessary before swallowing. "You're right. Getting involved is not something I'm comfortable with."

"Autumn is not only our employee—she's our friend," I said. "And the only way she will feel safe enough to come back to the bakery is if the real murderer is caught or we prove Florence's death was self-inflicted. If the sheriff isn't able to manage that on his own, we could lose both Autumn and the bakery."

Dottie's gaze dropped to the table as she thought on my words. "When you put it that way, how can I refuse?" She looked at me. "Not because it's our responsibility, mind you. I still don't like the idea of us interfering. But not helping people we care about—that feels worse."

I almost fell on the floor in surprise, and then Lars really would need to call the paramedics. Dottie was always so hands off when it came to anything regarding law enforcement. There had been too many times during her career when innocent people had gotten caught in the crossfire—not always literally—but they had made a situation worse than it had needed to be.

All in the spirit of helping, which was exactly what we were doing now.

"Thank you," I started. "I—"

Dottie interrupted me. "If there is anything that indicates Autumn is guilty, you have to promise me we'll do the right thing and turn her in." She paused. "I do care about Autumn, and if she is innocent, I will do everything in my power to protect her. But if she's guilty, I won't stop Sheriff Hart from doing his job."

That might not have sounded very promising to some people, but it was more than what I had been expecting.

"Deal," I said. "No harboring murderers allowed, but no allowing innocent people to be punished either."

Where to go from here?

We knew that Florence had likely been killed with her own knife before she'd had the opportunity to enter the water, but that was about it.

"We need an inside person," I said. "We don't know anything about what really happened that night, and we have no idea what, if anything, the sheriff has discovered."

Dottie raised a shoulder. "So, let's pay him a visit. A little quid pro quo. It'll be better than sneaking around his back. We could form some kind of a symbiotic relationship."

I hesitated. "You trust him for something like that?"

Dottie wiped a bit of soup off her chin. "No, but he might appreciate the help from a former big city cop if he hasn't encountered a homicide before. Besides, do you have a better idea?"

We had already talked with Isaac and found out everything he knew, which wasn't much. From talking with him,

I had initially concluded that Florence's death had been self-inflicted, but that had seemed out of character for her. That was, until we'd learned about the incident involving Clarissa's son. Now I didn't know what to think.

Jessie, for all the gossip she collected in a day, didn't know much about the actual murder. She seemed to know where Autumn was hiding out, which was comforting but not helpful in exonerating her.

Who else would know about what had gone on last evening?

No one.

Isaac had said there had been no other divers out. He'd been alone.

"Clarissa," I said. "Why don't we talk to her? If Florence didn't kill herself, Clarissa had every reason to."

Dottie gave me a skeptical eye as she stabbed at the last couple of stubborn bites of her salad. "Confronting the best suspect we have, straight on? That seems dangerous and could make us lose the element of surprise. If the sheriff doesn't know about her and Florence's past, she may think she's in the clear. But then if we show up snooping around, and it really was her, she disappears and we never see her again. Which means—"

"That Autumn takes the fall," I finished for her. "Okay. So, we save Clarissa until we have concrete evidence she could have been involved." I racked my brain trying to come up with anyone else we could visit, other than the sheriff. I wasn't keen on being on the receiving end of his questioning quite so soon after our encounter this morning.

I didn't come up with anyone else.

So, Dottie and I sat in silence as we finished our food. I was about to admit defeat and agree to pay the sheriff a visit when the diner door opened. And in walked none other than the sheriff himself. He moved toward the counter, but then his gaze landed on us, and he switched directions.

"If you're looking for Autumn, we can't help you," I told him as he approached, forgetting that we were supposed to be on the offensive and not the defensive. "This is a sisters-only luncheon."

Sheriff Hart seemed taken aback by my direct approach, but he nodded. "That's all right. I think I got what I needed from talking with her this morning."

Oh. Either the sheriff was putting on a show or Autumn wasn't as prime a suspect as we'd thought she was.

"That may be, but there are other things we need to discuss," Dottie said. She scooted over and patted the seat next to her. "Let's have a chat."

It seemed we were doing this now. I supposed it was better than on the sheriff's home turf, even if I was still unsure this was the right course of action. It was all we had, though. Autumn may not be a prime suspect, but she wasn't yet off the hook.

Sheriff Hart glanced between the two of us like he

thought it might be a trick. "If you honestly think I have the budget to pay you for information—"

Dottie laughed. "No, no. We're not after anything like that." And then she patted the seat again.

When neither of us spoke further, the sheriff gave in and sat down.

"We both have a common goal," Dottie said. "To catch Florence's killer. I'm assuming this is your first homicide case. Is that correct?"

Sheriff Hart hesitated but then nodded.

"Wonderful. We'd like to help you," Dottie said with a smile. For someone who hadn't wanted to get involved with solving this murder in the first place, she was a natural. It made me wonder what else she'd been able to expertly fake while we were growing up together.

Sheriff Hart drummed his fingers on the table. "And how exactly do you think you can do that?"

"We were thinking of a quid pro quo arrangement," I said. "We tell you what we know, you return the favor, that kind of thing."

Dottie shot me a glare, but I couldn't figure out why. Until the sheriff smiled and turned to me.

"And what exactly is it that you know?" he asked. "Because if you know something about a murder investigation that you are refusing to tell me, that would be obstruction of justice. And that's illegal."

Oh. I'd been around long enough that he didn't need to spell it out for me. It could be a scare tactic, but the way

Dottie was looking at me—like she could murder me—we'd just lost our edge.

"How is that illegal?" I asked, feigning innocence. "I don't know what is important to an investigation and what's not. What I do know is that these are amazing enchiladas, and they are the special today, so you'll want to ask Lars to get you a plate."

Sheriff Hart fixed me with his stare.

"Fine," I relented. "We really don't know where Autumn is, but we do know that this might not be a murder case at all. It could be suicide."

That should be enough to keep him off our backs for a while, and if he could prove it was suicide, then Autumn was free. Win-win.

That was wishful thinking, and I should have known from the beginning that that was not how this was going to go. Nothing ever worked out quite that well for me.

The sheriff sat silently for a moment, studying me. He looked between Dottie and me and then released a long sigh. "Florence Whitlock did not die from suicide. In fact, she didn't even die from the knife wound."

Wow, my strategy had worked. He was actually sharing real information with us.

Judging by Dottie's expression, she was just as shocked as I was.

"However," he continued, "you aren't going to like what we did find."

Oh. Crap.

I was tempted to cover my ears so I couldn't hear what he had to say next, but he was too fast.

"Florence was poisoned," the sheriff said. "And we discovered the source."

I already thought I knew what he was going to say, and I squeezed my eyes shut, as if that would make it all go away.

"It was your dacquoise. A pastry from your bakery is what killed Florence Whitlock."

11

Nope. This was not happening.

I refused to believe it.

Our pastry chef did not kill Florence. Autumn was not guilty. Our bakery wasn't going to shut down after only one evening of being open, and we were all going to live happily ever after.

I'd promised Dottie that if Autumn was guilty, we'd hand her over to the sheriff. I realized I'd only said it to make my sister feel better—I'd never give Autumn up, even if all evidence pointed to her. It was a good thing that Jessie hadn't entrusted us with Autumn's location. Now we didn't have to lie.

Which Dottie wouldn't have done, but I'd have lied straight to the sheriff's face without an ounce of guilt about it.

Dottie had been stunned into silence—a rarity—and

after a few moments, I spoke up. "The whole town was at our bakery last night. Half of them ate the dacquoise, and no one else ended up dead."

"Correct," the sheriff said slowly, like he'd thought of that. "But no one else ate from *her* dacquoise. The one that Florence purchased."

"Well, no, but how would Autumn know that Florence was going to purchase a dacquoise, let alone how many slices and which ones they would be?" I asked. "Autumn wasn't even behind the counter selling the pastries. She was mingling and answering any questions people had about the various desserts we had out."

"Right," the sheriff said. And then he just stared at me, like I was supposed to be understanding something that I'd apparently missed.

"So...what's the problem?"

Dottie hadn't needed the sheriff's help to interpret his silence. She slammed her hands down on the table with such force that I nearly had a heart attack. Everyone in the diner looked our way.

"Don't you dare try to pin this on Jo," Dottie said. "Look at her. Do you really think she's capable of something like this? She believes everyone has good inside them, much to her detriment. Her hair has that damn-near blinding shade of pink in it, and she believes that breakfast should be eaten three times a day, every day, because breakfast food is the only food worth eating."

She glanced at my plate. "Unless you offer her Mexican or Thai food. Then she makes an exception."

I glanced between Dottie and the sheriff. "Wait, you don't mean... You couldn't actually think that—"

"Yes," Dottie said, turning her fierce gaze on me. "Sheriff Hart thinks that you poisoned Florence. You were the one selling the pastries and were the only one behind the counter. This would have been after Florence's insults, after your speech when you came to Autumn's rescue, and you would have had plenty of opportunity to slip something into Florence's dacquoise amid all the commotion of the party."

I'd thought Dottie was supposed to be on my side, but she'd just laid out a really convincing argument about why, and how, I could be the killer.

I let out a single barking laugh. "Right, because I have poison just sitting around so I can sprinkle it on people's purchases as I see fit."

The sheriff remained silent. I could tell he hated this and he was miserable even having this discussion, but that wouldn't be enough to keep him from locking me away. When I was younger, I'd told Dottie that going to jail should be one of those 'everyone does it once in their lifetime' kind of experiences, just to rile her up a little. This had been after I'd stolen an ugly little ceramic frog from a store in the mall and I'd had to sneak it back in to return it.

But I had meant getting arrested for something silly

that would see me released the next day. Not for something like this. Not for murder.

At my age, I'd die before ever being released.

"What was the poison?" Dottie asked. I could tell she'd
compartmentalized and emotion was no longer part of the
discussion. Her angry outburst—that Dottie was gone. We
were back to practical, no-nonsense Dorothy.

The sheriff looked between the two of us, as if he were
trying to discern if we really didn't know. "Cyanide," he
eventually said.

She didn't look surprised, instead giving a thoughtful
nod. "It makes sense. Even if there was a slight almond
taste or smell, it was in a dessert where entire layers were
made of nuts. Florence wouldn't have thought anything
of it."

I raised my hand. "Um, sorry, but where would I get
cyanide from, and why would I just happen to have some
on hand?"

From Sheriff Hart's blank look, I could tell he hadn't
gotten that far. But regardless of where I'd procured the
poison, he had enough evidence to arrest me.

The dacquoise. All eight pieces of it. Seven of them to
kill Florence, and one to put me in prison.

Jessie and Adeline still sat in their booth, talking and
laughing as if nothing bad could ever happen to them.
And it probably wouldn't.

One thing was for sure—I wasn't going to put on a
show for them, or anyone else, kicking and screaming

about how I was innocent. With Dottie on the case, this would all be resolved soon. I hoped. She had a unique view on justice—mainly that it applied to everyone, including her relations. And if she at any point was convinced of my guilt—well, I hoped it didn't get to that point.

Sheriff Hart hadn't ordered anything for himself yet. He'd likely planned on a quick lunch before heading over to the bakery to deliver the bad news, but that had changed when he'd seen us.

On the bright side, I wouldn't have to walk back to the bakery now. It made me sad to think that Dottie would have to make the trek alone.

I stood from the booth. "Come on, you two. Sheriff Hart, please drop my sister off at the bakery on our way to your station. Her knees have had to work hard enough for one day."

They both looked at me in surprise.

"You're not seriously considering going with him," Dottie said. "He can't arrest you—"

The sheriff interrupted her. "I can, and I will." He paused. "But I'd rather not do it here, if you don't mind."

"There you go, Dottie. The sheriff and I are on the same wavelength." I gestured toward the door. "Come on, I don't want to put this off longer than I have to." And then I stopped by the counter, left enough money for both my and Dottie's meals, and walked out the door. That left the sheriff and Dottie scrambling to catch up.

"You don't have to do this," Dottie said. "You have rights, you know."

I gave her an empathetic smile. "And he has probable cause. I trust you to get me out of this mess. You were the best cop on your force, and you're the best cop we have here in Starlight Ridge."

"I don't wear the badge anymore," Dottie said, sending Sheriff Hart an anxious glance, like she wondered if she really could prove I hadn't killed Florence.

I rested my hand on her arm and forced her to look me in the eyes. Her face was weathered, likely due to all the time spent under stress while she had been a cop. Time hadn't been kind to her. But she was my sister, and I trusted her. "You can do this. You need to. Or else you're going to find yourself running that bakery all by yourself, and you know that cat of yours is just going to make it harder. Did you know that she sneaks into the kitchen anytime she gets a chance and Autumn routinely needs to kick her off the oven? That has to be some sort of health code violation."

Dottie's lips twitched up. "Not to mention dangerous. I'll take care of the Skittles problem, I promise."

I gave a single satisfied nod, then turned to the sheriff. "You don't have to put the handcuffs on me, do you? I bruise easily."

The sheriff shook his head and rubbed his eyebrows. "No, I don't."

"Good." I moved to get into the back seat, and he

cocked an eyebrow. I paused. "Aren't I supposed to sit back here behind the window so I don't stab you or something while we drive?"

That earned a smile. "Were you planning on stabbing me?"

"No."

"Then you can sit up front with me. We'll let your sister sit in the back."

Dottie opened her mouth to protest, but I shouted, "Too late, he said I can sit in the front." And I slid into the front seat.

Both Dottie and I knew that she could never win in a foot race, so she didn't even try.

As we drove, Dottie whispered from behind me, "I wasn't used to having a roommate before we moved in together at the bakery. Now, I don't think I'll be able to sleep knowing you aren't in the next room."

I was sorry I wouldn't be there for Dottie, but knowing that she needed me as much as I needed her—even on my way to being arrested, I'd never felt more at peace.

12

I 'd expected we'd have a long drive to wherever the sheriff's office was, but instead, after dropping Dottie off, he stopped at an old building just off the boardwalk.

"What are we doing here?" It looked like the kind of place where people were tortured in movies. "You going to tie me up and leave me here but tell people I died in custody and then cover up the crime, is that it?"

Sheriff Hart shook his head. "You watch too many crime dramas." He turned to me. "Logistically, being sheriff here is a nightmare. I'm in charge of three towns, but I technically only work out of one of them. You haven't had a sheriff stationed here in Starlight Ridge in at least two decades, because you haven't needed one. And then you manage to get two murders in less than a year."

He nodded to the old building in front of us. "You do have a station, and there is a holding cell in there, but that's about it. Dusty furniture and no technology to speak of. I can't work like that. But to have you thirty minutes away means I'll be driving back and forth constantly, and you'll often be alone with my deputy. If he gets a call, then you'll really be on your own, and with no bathroom. We can't have that."

I grinned. "Sheriff Hart, that almost sounded like you care about me."

He laughed, but it was more of a sad laugh that made me want to put my arm around his shoulders and tell him it was all going to be all right. "Of course I do. Even if you were a hardened criminal, I would still care. I have empathy for what a lot of these guys go through, and the road they traveled to get where they are."

Whenever I saw Dottie in her cop uniform, she'd always appeared to be above the rest of us mere mortals. Not that she'd meant to, but it had changed how she would act, her demeanor—it changed everything.

But to see the sheriff with his badge and being so vulnerable—well, it might have been more than just his lovely green eyes that gave me a soft spot for the guy.

"I hope your mama is proud of you," I said, patting his arm. "You're a good man."

The sheriff's gaze dropped. "I like to think she would have been. She passed away when I was a teenager. Drunk driver."

"Did they ever catch the guy?"

"Nope."

Cops usually had a story about why they joined the force. For some it was as simple as their dad was a cop, their grandpa was a cop, and now they're a cop.

For others, like Sheriff Hart or Dottie, it wasn't so simple.

"I'm sorry you didn't get that closure," I said.

He cleared his throat and straightened in his seat. "It is what it is."

"I can be your mama," I said brightly. "Never had kids of my own, but I could figure it out."

That really did make Sheriff Hart laugh, and this time it was genuine. "I appreciate the gesture, but how about if we figure out what we're going to do with you first?"

I raised a shoulder. "You could let me go."

His smile dipped, and I wished it would return. "You know I can't do that. Everything points to you, Jo. I don't know you well, and this sweet grandma routine you got going on—it could be you playing me for a sucker." He paused, then mumbled, "It wouldn't be the first time." The bitterness that laced the last sentence, I had heard it before.

"Let me guess," I said. "You're divorced. No kids. And she ran off with your best friend."

He harrumphed. "You got the best friend part wrong. It was her boss."

I grimaced. "I don't know why, but that feels worse. Is it, though? The best friend thing would be more of a betrayal, and you'd lose both your wife and your friend. But the boss thing—that's an abuse of power."

The sheriff didn't look like he enjoyed the direction the conversation had taken, and he opened his door. "Let's see how bad your station is, then I'll decide where to put you."

Where to put me. Like I was an odd trinket picked up on vacation that didn't really fit with any of the decor, but you'd bought it, so now you felt obligated to do something with it.

I watched as the sheriff pulled out a key and tried the lock.

The man was not at all what he'd first seemed. An empathetic divorcé who had lost his mother as a teenager but was still willing to arrest an old woman, even if he didn't like it. To be fair, he was treating me more like he was putting me up for a few days at a hotel than arresting me for murder.

I was unsure how to make sense of all that, but I was determined to figure out the enigma that was Sheriff Hart.

"The lock was rusty, but I got it," he said, gesturing for me to follow him. As we entered the station, I coughed from all the dust in the air.

"When was the last time someone was in here?" I asked, holding my sleeve over my nose.

Sheriff Hart glanced back as he searched the walls for a light switch. "No idea. Probably not since the sheriff left, maybe twenty years ago? Give or take."

Yeah, that seemed about right, considering the state of

things. Old computers sat on even older desks, garbage cans hadn't been emptied, and paperwork that had never been filed cluttered the area.

"Did the last sheriff leave in a hurry?" I asked. They had to have, or else why leave all this stuff here? Even though it was worthless now, I was sure that back then it had had some value.

Sheriff Hart found the switch, but nothing happened when he flipped it on. He laughed and buried his head in his hands. "I don't know why I expected the electricity to still work in this place. It's not like anyone has been paying the bill."

"It was a fair assumption," I said. "In the movies, the lights always come on in old abandoned buildings."

The sheriff placed his hands on his hips and surveyed the area. "I think it's fair to say that I can't have you staying in a place like this."

"No, you can't," I agreed. "What if you put me on something like house arrest? That way I can't leave town without you knowing, but you don't have to be inconvenienced by that long drive out to your office."

Sheriff Hart lit up, like that was a possibility, but it morphed into a shake of the head. "I would love if we could, but the legal system doesn't work like that. There's paperwork and rules and regulations, and we certainly don't have the budget for something as high tech as an ankle bracelet. No, they'd never go for it."

A simple no would have sufficed.

"I could stay at your station but accompany you into Starlight Ridge each day," I suggested. "You know, be your traveling deputy of sorts."

Sheriff Hart started laughing, until he realized I was serious. "You want to come with me and investigate the murder that you may have committed?"

I nodded. "Sure. I won't go near evidence, the crime scene, or anything I could potentially tamper with. But you could use the company, and I need someplace to stay that doesn't have rats."

"This office doesn't have—"

I nodded toward the desk nearest him, where a rat was munching on something that might have been food twenty years ago—it was difficult to tell at this point.

Sheriff Hart scurried over to where I stood, putting as much distance as possible between himself and the rodent. "Point taken."

"So, what is it going to be, Sheriff?" I asked, sticking out my hand. "Partners?"

His expression held multiple emotions at once, evidence of the conflicting thoughts he was likely experiencing. Leaving me alone in another town while he worked here in Starlight Ridge wasn't a great option, but, admittedly, neither was taking me out to investigate Florence's murder.

His gaze finally settled on me, and I could tell he'd made his decision. "All right," he said. "You can come on the job with me for one day. If you can manage to stay out of trouble, we can discuss a second day."

I beamed and puffed out my chest. "You can trust me, Sheriff. I'll be the best partner you've ever had."

He winced, and I could tell he was already regretting his decision. "Once again, you are not my partner. You are a suspect in a murder investigation who happens to be following me around for the day. You have to be within my sight at all times."

"What if I'm in the bathroom?"

He released a groan of exasperation. "Why do people always ask about the bathroom? Of course I'm not going to go in there with you, but you can only use bathrooms that have no windows."

That seemed sensible. "I've never understood bathrooms that have windows. I mean, why? You don't need to enjoy a view of the outdoors while you're doing your business, and you certainly don't need the random people who happen to be outside enjoying the view. Just get a can of air freshener, and you're set."

"Do you always talk this much?" he asked, walking out the open door. He waited for me to exit so he could lock back up.

"Sometimes. It depends."

Sheriff Hart twisted the key, then turned to me. "On what?"

"If I have a captive audience."

13

M y first night in a jail cell wasn't as bad as I'd expected. If I had been in a bigger city where there were other inmates, I could see how things might get a little dicey. I'd seen a few episodes of *Orange is the New Black*, and that had been enough. But it turned out that if you're in a small town where the only people that hang out at the sheriff's office are troubled teenagers and alcoholics, you're treated pretty well.

When I arrived, a cot was the only thing available to sleep on. After the sheriff left for the evening, I asked Sheriff Hart's deputy, Randy, if he would mind getting me something a bit more comfortable, maybe a blow-up mattress with a set of sheets and a different pillow. My body needed better support now that it didn't recover as quickly as it used to.

Randy came back with something even better—an

actual mattress. It was queen-size, complete with box spring and fresh linens. I felt like I was in a fancy hotel, being waited on hand and foot the way I was. Unfortunately, there wasn't an extra blanket and my feet got a little cold during the night, but I told Randy not to feel bad about it, I'd still bring something back from the bakery the following day.

Now that I thought about it, some of the preferential treatment may have been because of some bribery on my part, but I liked to believe that it mostly had to do with what a nice young man Randy was.

After getting me settled, he ran over to their version of Lars' diner and got me my favorite comfort food, French toast. He then turned on the TV so I could watch *Ted Lasso* with him, after which we had a lively debate on if there would be a season four. I had to say that may have been the best show I'd ever seen, and that was saying something because I'd loved watching classic shows like *Hogan's Heroes* when I was younger.

But it was just that good.

When Sheriff Hart came in the following morning and saw the mattress, he was less accommodating. He stared at it, the bed already made and the sheets tucked in, for a full minute before saying anything.

"Randy," he barked, "the only thing you're missing is the cross-stitched wall hanging and the potpourri."

Randy, the poor guy, immediately jumped from his seat. "Yes, sir. Right away."

And then he ran from the room, faster than Sheriff Hart could correct him.

"I was being sarcastic," he said to me, though I thought he was mostly talking to himself and wondering how he'd ended up with a deputy like Randy.

"I know you were," I said, "but I do appreciate all the efforts he's gone to to make me comfortable. Honestly, this cot was invented for war criminals, not old women."

The sheriff rubbed his eyes. "We don't bring in new bed sheets and box springs for suspects in murder investigations."

"But I told Randy I didn't kill Florence, and he believes me. He also believed me when I told him it takes me a full fifteen minutes to get out of bed in the morning. I mean, honestly, I need to do something because my back is going to give out on me one of these days. Maybe some physical therapy would help. Or a chiropractor. Do you use a chiropractor? I've never been, and some people don't consider them real doctors, but I'd be willing to give one a try."

Sheriff Hart remained standing with his head bent, no doubt questioning his life choices, before his gaze finally found me. "Have you had breakfast yet?" he asked, his voice soft.

"Yes. Randy was kind enough to bring me some waffles and eggs. It was the perfect start to the day."

Sheriff Hart laughed in disbelief. "Yes, very good. Glad we could do that for you." He then unlocked the cell door and gestured for me to exit. "Come on, time for our workday to start."

"You know, at first I wasn't sure of the arrangement we made," I said. "But I think it's turning out quite well. And I have a good feeling about what we'll discover today in Starlight Ridge."

That got the sheriff's attention. He had been shutting the cell door but stopped and turned toward me. "Do you know something, Jo?"

I gave him a quizzical look. "No. Should I?"

"When you say you have a good feeling about today—"

I laughed and waved a hand through the air. "Oh, no, it's just a little something I picked up from my older sister, Beatrice. She always had a sixth sense about things, and she really could tell if something good or bad was heading our way. One time she got this funny look about her, and she told me I needed to walk to school rather than taking the bus. It was two miles in one direction, but I trusted Beatrice and left thirty minutes early so I could get there on time."

When I didn't continue right away, the sheriff finished shutting the cell door, then turned to me. "Well, what happened? Did the bus get into an accident?"

I shrugged. "No idea. But if I would have gotten on that bus, it wouldn't have been good, I'll tell you that much. I never doubted Beatrice and her gift."

Sheriff Hart gave me a funny look. "Or maybe she was messing with her sister and just wanted to see you walk two miles to school," he said, then motioned for me to follow him outside. Sheriff Hart was an unbeliever, but no matter. I would have been one too if it weren't for Beatrice.

WHEN WE REACHED STARLIGHT RIDGE, the sheriff pulled over next to the boardwalk, his gaze settling on the ocean. I could see Isaac at his lifeguard station, keeping watch over a couple of boys playing in the ocean waves.

"I never get tired of it," Sheriff Hart said, his voice wistful. "The water. There's something about it that's so calming. And then someone pulls a dead body out of it."

"Isaac didn't pull Florence out of the ocean," I said, surprised he didn't know otherwise. "He found her on the beach. I figured you knew."

That was what I got for assuming. And then there I went letting the sheriff arrest me for something I hadn't done when he didn't even have all the facts.

His gaze snapped to me, surprise in his features. "He said he found Florence and tried to give her CPR. I suppose he didn't specifically say he pulled her out of the water, but considering the wetsuit and everything, I guess I thought—" He squeezed his eyes shut. When he reopened them, his features relaxed. "It doesn't matter when we already know how she died."

"Well, I think it matters a great deal," I said. "Especially considering the empty beer bottles that were found next to her."

"Isaac mentioned those," the sheriff said, his words slow, as if he were trying to decipher what I was getting at. "Why do they matter? It wouldn't be the first time someone has had a couple of beers before heading out for a night dive, dangerous or not."

"Did you check her blood alcohol level when you read the toxicology report?"

Sheriff Hart didn't answer right away, which meant no. "I stopped reading when I saw the cyanide," he murmured. "When you see a poison like that, you don't need anything else. It would have killed her in a matter of minutes, if not seconds."

Which meant that Florence wouldn't have been drinking beer on the beach in her wetsuit. Because she would have already been dead.

"Sheriff," I started, realizing what that meant.

He sighed. "Yes, I know. It means she was dead before she even arrived at the beach. The poisoned dacquoise was back in her kitchen. Someone placed her on the beach."

I raised my hand, as if I were back in school. "I hate to point out the obvious, but I don't have the strength, nor the stamina, to carry a body down to the beach."

Sheriff Hart studied me. "You could have had help."

I laughed. "Not from Dottie."

"Autumn is pretty strong. As is Jessie. You seem like you're close with both of them."

That made me laugh even harder. "You think that Autumn, Jessie, and I dragged a body that was already heavier than normal because of the wetsuit down to the beach. And why would we place the empty beer bottles?"

"To throw me off track," he said. "Either that or they weren't even hers."

This man was impossible. One minute, he seemed like he wanted to help me out, to the point where I'd offered to adopt him. The next, he was giving crazy theories, trying to justify how I could have been the killer.

"Do you really believe that?" I asked.

He pushed open the car door and stood, then leaned on the hood, his gaze scanning the boardwalk. "No, I don't. The more people involved in a crime, the harder it is to cover up." He turned to me. "Or maybe Autumn and Jessie didn't help you at all. It could have been someone who is strong enough to do it on his own and gullible enough to assist a helpless old woman."

He was nodding now, like he'd figured it all out, and it was infuriating.

"First off, I'm not some helpless old woman," I said, frowning and placing a hand on my hip. The gesture only made him smile, which made me more upset. "Second, where am I going to find a random man who is willing to plant a body for me?"

Sheriff Hart didn't answer right away, his fingers drumming the top of the car.

"What about him?" he asked, pointing toward the beach.

I pushed myself out of the car and looked in the direction he'd indicated. A man was walking along the beach, and I instantly recognized him.

"You think Coach David helped me?" I asked with an incredulous laugh. "He is certainly strong enough, but we don't have that kind of rapport."

The sheriff looked to me. "So, you know him."

"Barely. Dottie and I took his parkour class a few days ago. And by that, I mean we turned up, did our best, and left early. It wasn't exactly our scene, if you know what I mean."

"Oh, right. You and Dottie were taking a parkour class. I guess that's what we're calling secret clandestine meetings nowadays."

"I'm not lying to you," I insisted. "Go ask him. He'll tell you. I've known him a grand total of thirty minutes and haven't seen him since."

Sheriff Hart studied me, like he was trying to figure out if I was messing with him, but then he pushed away from the car and walked over to David, who had turned toward the boardwalk. They began talking, but I couldn't hear enough to know what was going on. I knew that the sheriff didn't want me interfering, but I needed to get close enough to overhear what was being said. I was the topic of conversation, after all. It was only right that I know what they were saying about me.

It turned out that close enough to hear was standing right next to them.

"Yeah, she's gutsy," David was saying. "Most people are tentative when they start out, but she really went for it."

He couldn't be talking about me, because that was not at all how that parkour class had gone.

I stopped just behind the sheriff's back, hoping he wouldn't realize I was there. Unfortunately, David had no problem seeing the old lady peeking from behind the sheriff's back.

"Tell him about the balance bar," David said, looking straight at me.

Sheriff Hart turned, his eyebrows furrowed in frustration. I gave him a weak smile and a small wave in return.

"I'd rather not talk about the balance bar," I said. "It's still giving me nightmares."

"Nonsense. You did great. It's quite difficult for someone of any age, not just you. And it takes months to get really good at it. If you come back every week, I know you'll master it, easy."

David had such faith in me, and I didn't understand why. I hadn't even been able to lift one foot without crashing to the ground, and I'd met every other exercise, including the warmups, with the same disastrous fervor.

"We'll see," I said, not wanting to commit to anything. Not only because I was unsure my pride could withstand it, but there was also the little issue of me still being a murder suspect.

"I did have one other question," Sheriff Hart started, turning back to Coach David, but then he paused and looked like he was having a difficult time figuring out how to ask it. When he glanced back at me with an annoyed expression, I realized what it was.

The sheriff didn't know how to ask David if he had helped me carry Florence's dead body down to the beach and stage it so it looked like she'd been killed with a diving knife, and my presence wasn't helping.

Yeah, that was going to be a tough one.

14

"Jo!"

I turned from Sheriff Hart and Coach David to see Autumn running full speed at me. She crashed into me, wrapped her arms around my neck, and gave me the longest, tightest hug I'd ever received.

"As soon as I heard what happened, I went straight to the bakery to check on Dorothy," she said. "I'm so sorry. If I hadn't run away, you wouldn't be in this mess." She released me and stepped back, looking me over. "Are you okay? The sheriff treat you all right?" She eyed him warily, still not trusting him, but at least she'd come out of hiding.

I laughed, overcome by her exuberance, and I was holding on to every minute of it. As much as I loved Dottie, she wasn't prone to show her emotions like Autumn did, and even though I knew Dottie loved me, sometimes I needed to feel it in more concrete ways.

"None of this is your fault," I said. "Where have you been?"

"The bed and breakfast. Jessie's been visiting and keeping me company, and in return, I've been teaching her some of my pastry techniques."

Of course. Not only had Jessie known where Autumn was, but now she was taking baking classes from her. That seemed about right.

I lowered my voice. "We need to talk, because something weird is going on. The dacquoise we sold to Florence was laced with cyanide."

She gave a vigorous nod. "Yes, I know. Dottie told me. How did you convince the sheriff that you didn't do it?"

Sheriff Hart had moved in closer. Apparently, this broke my promise of not tampering with the case. "She hasn't convinced me," he said. "In fact, she's only here under strict observation, because..."

He couldn't seem to find the words, so I finished his thought for him.

"Because he felt bad for me. He didn't like the thought of me being locked up all day and not always having access to help if I needed it. For a minute there, I thought he cared about me."

The sheriff turned his gaze on me. "Now, wait a minute. Just because I don't let you run around and do whatever you want doesn't mean I don't care. But the fact is that you are a suspect in a murder investigation. You need to cut me some slack and understand things from my point of view."

Coach David's jaw went slack. "There's been some kind of mistake. Jo couldn't have done something like that."

The sheriff turned to him. "You've known her all of thirty minutes. How would you know what she's capable of?"

"Because I know people," David said, jutting out his chin. A thrill ran up my spine at the way this man was protecting my good name when he really didn't have to.

"So, tell me, David," Sheriff Hart said. "You know people. Who is known for their strength in this town?"

David tilted his head, like he was trying to figure out why the sheriff would want to know, but he must have come up empty. "Other than me, it's my assistant coaches, Eliza and Peter. It's why I recruited them for the parkour class. When spotting other people who are doing risky moves, you have to be able to support someone else's weight."

My breath escaped in a quick whoosh, and I squeezed my eyes shut. I really wished he wouldn't have said it like that.

"Strong enough to carry another person's weight, you say. Even dead weight?" the sheriff asked.

David's eyes widened slightly. He knew what he'd inadvertently done, but it was too late. "Yes," he said, his words now slow and calculated. "If someone were to have a medical emergency, we would need to be able to move them into a safe space."

Sheriff Hart smiled. "Thank you. That's all I needed to

know. Can I get your phone number, in case I have any further questions?"

David didn't look like he wanted to hand it over, and understandably so, but he did as he was asked.

The sheriff said goodbye to David and Autumn and motioned for me to follow him back to his car.

I gave Autumn a small wave and whispered, "This will all be cleared up soon enough. Let Dottie know I'm okay."

And then I hurried after the sheriff.

"Anything about that exchange strike you as unusual?" he asked as I slid into the car and fastened my seatbelt.

"Just because someone can lift dead weight doesn't mean they are guilty of moving a dead body," I said, already anticipating where he was going with this.

The sheriff was silent for a beat. "I meant that he seemed to hold you in such high regard, particularly for someone you claim barely knows you."

"High regard?" I snorted. "He has faith that I can master not falling on my face, so I suppose if that's high regard, then sure, why not."

"He also vehemently denied you could have anything to do with the murder, even though he has no knowledge of the facts or the people involved."

I turned to him. "You can't possibly be saying that you think Coach David was involved."

"You two seemed awfully comfortable for not knowing each other long. About the same age too. You sure you haven't wandered down by the parkour class every once in a while, check out the view? Maybe get to know the hand-some coach on a more personal level."

Sheriff Hart was goading me now, and I didn't like it. "Stop the car," I said. He didn't. The only thing he did was look at me like I was crazy for thinking I was the one in charge. "I said, stop the car," I repeated, louder. "I'm serious. I can't be here with you. Not when you're going to treat me like this." I was near tears, but I wasn't going to give him the satisfaction of seeing them fall.

The sheriff seemed taken aback by my outburst, and he pulled the car over. "Jo, I didn't mean—"

"Yes, you did," I said, unstrapping my seatbelt and pushing my door open. "Because I'm a suspect. That's all I am to you. You can talk about empathy and compassion all you want, but I don't like being badgered like this. You're after information, and since I'm not going anywhere, you're going to push me and keep asking questions. You're trying to trick me into giving up information I don't have. And I'm not going to stand for it."

I got out of the car, slammed the door shut, and stalked off toward the beach, not caring about the rules I was supposed to be following.

I'd thought it could be fun to be in jail for a day. Now I could say I'd done it, and I just wanted to go back to my old life. The one where I was opening up a bakery with my seventy-year-old sister and trying to sing along to Autumn's music, even though I didn't know the lyrics. The life where I could come and go as I pleased without worrying if I was going to die in a cold cell for something I didn't do.

Maybe the sheriff hadn't meant to badger me—maybe he really was trying to help. But if he thought me innocent, he sure had a funny way of going about it.

I wrapped my arms around my waist, looking out over the water. It was so beautiful. So calming, just as the sheriff had said.

So, why had it brought such trouble into my life as of late?

"Jo," Sheriff Hart said behind me. "You have to understand that you could go to trial with the evidence I have. If the truth is still out there—and you truly are innocent—trust me, you want me asking all the questions. Because that's all I want. The truth."

I spun to face him. "I won't be tried for Florence's murder. Dottie won't allow it. You haven't found traces of cyanide in my bakery. You haven't found evidence I've moved a body. The only thing I'm guilty of is hiring a woman who makes dacquoise that is so incredible, a woman bought eight slices of it. And that was after she'd already eaten three slices at our grand opening. You have no motive for me. You have nothing. I've gone along with your little game, like it was a grand adventure. But I'm over it. And I want to go home."

This time the tears really did come. I slapped them away, but they didn't pay any attention to me, running as freely as they pleased.

Sheriff Hart collapsed onto the sand. "You're right. I don't have the answers I need. I've never investigated a murder before. The most I usually do is call parents to tell them their kid was caught smoking weed with their friends and to come pick them up from the station. What makes it even harder is that I don't know anyone in this town. No one trusts me. And I feel lost. I've gone where the evidence has directed me, and it led me to you. But my gut says I'm wrong. So, what am I supposed to do with that?"

It was hard to stay angry with the sheriff when he looked like a sad and scared little puppy.

I sat in the sand next to him.

"You follow the evidence, like you said. Yes, Florence was killed by cyanide that somehow found its way into our dacquoise, but there is no proof that it was administered in my bakery. What the evidence does tell you is that Florence was dead before she arrived on that beach, and that there was no way I could have carried her. So, if we follow that line of logic, you need to release me from custody and pick up the thread where you left off."

I gave him my best puppy dog eyes, making him laugh.

"You know, if I didn't know any better, I'd say you were closer to eight years old than sixty-eight."

Good, that had been what I'd been going for.

Sheriff Hart was quiet for a moment before turning to me. "Jo, you could have poisoned the dacquoise, and someone else could have moved the body. But you're right. Even though you had opportunity, I have no physical evidence tying you to the poison." He paused. "I am letting you go. You can sleep in your own bed tonight. But you need to know that this investigation is far from over. If I come knocking on your door or call your bakery—even outside business hours—I expect you to answer."

I crossed my heart with my fingers but then released a little gasp.

"What? Did you think of something?" the sheriff asked, his expression alert.

I shook my head. "No. I mean yes, but nothing to do with your case. I promised to bring back some pastries for Randy tonight. He's going to be so disappointed. Would you mind delivering them for me?"

Sheriff Hart looked at me like I'd gone insane. "That's how you got all that luxury treatment, by bribing Randy with baked goods? And all the while, I'm trying to solve a murder."

"I didn't bribe him," I said, immediately defensive. "I don't do stuff like that. Bribing an officer of the law is illegal. I merely offered him pastries as a kind gesture after he helped me out."

From the expression on the sheriff's face, he didn't think that was much better.

But then he said, "Only if you send enough for me too."

I shot him an amused smile. "Isn't that bribery?"

Caught in his own trap, he looked at me guiltily, and then said, "No, it's a kind gesture."

The sheriff could be funny when he wanted to be. I let

out a barking laugh. "All right, pastries for two it is. Hopefully now that Autumn isn't worried that she's a suspect, she'll be back to baking so I can deliver on that promise." I tried to push myself up but realized getting up from sand was even more difficult than from my bakery floor, which had already been impossible. I held up a hand.

Sheriff Hart stood, then pulled me up. "You're mistaken," he said, as we worked our way back to the boardwalk. "About Autumn no longer being a suspect. At this point, everyone is."

15

I shouldn't have been surprised that Autumn was still a suspect and that, in fact, the whole town was. Most of them had been at the grand opening where the fatal dacquoise had been sold. But even I knew that you couldn't throw out a net large enough to cover an entire town and expect to catch a murderer. More likely than not, you'd catch everything, and everyone, except the one person you needed.

To his credit, even though Sheriff Hart was casting a wide net, it seemed he was at least trying to narrow down his suspect list. Unfortunately, that meant that all the parkour coaches were now at the top of it. And I was fairly certain my position hadn't budged much either.

I'd only been to one parkour class, and I wasn't even sure it counted since I had left early, but I did feel an obligation to at least warn the coaches that they needed to be careful for the next few days. From what little I'd seen of them, I liked the coaches and felt they did a lot of good for the community. And right now, anything they did or said could be used against them, as innocent as it may seem in other contexts.

The moment I stepped into the bakery, however, all thoughts of the parkour coaches disappeared into a haze of baked meringue, sugar, and cream.

I was home.

Except, even though it smelled like home, no one was here. The OPEN sign was bright in the window, but no one was behind the counter. I pushed down my disappointment. I'd called to let Dottie know I'd been released and had expected her to be waiting with open arms.

"It smells amazing in here," I called.

And then Dottie and Autumn emerged from the kitchen, holding a dacquoise cake with a single candle stuck in the middle, while singing, "Happy getting-out-of-prison day to you."

I clapped my hands together, grinning so wide, it hurt my cheeks. "You two are the best," I said, then blew the candle out. As soon as Dottie set the dacquoise down on the counter, I gave her a big hug. "Thank you," I repeated over and over.

"How was it?" Dottie asked, pulling away. "I've heard the food is awful and they make you sleep on a cot."

"It actually wasn't bad," I said. "The sheriff's deputy is a sweetheart and brought me in a nice mattress and let me watch *Ted Lasso* with him. He also brought my favorite foods from their local diner. Don't tell Lars this, but their diner has better French toast. Oh, and the sheriff will be stopping by within the hour to pick up a few pastries for them to enjoy at the station. Just my way of saying thank you."

I expected Dottie to be happy for me. Instead, her lips parted in surprise, and then her eyebrows dipped.

"I've been worried sick since he drove off with you," Dottie said. "I couldn't sleep, imagining you on a hard cot, probably crying yourself to sleep. And it turns out that you were at a five-star luxury hotel, being waited on hand and foot. And we're giving pastries to the sheriff and his deputy, no less, as a thank you."

Now that I looked at Dottie closer, she did look like she could use some rest. Large dark bags rested under her bloodshot eyes.

"I'm sorry, Dottie. I didn't mean for you to worry. If it's any consolation, them releasing me doesn't mean I'm entirely off the hook, it merely means they don't have enough evidence to hold me. For now."

"What do you mean, for now?" Dottie asked.

"He thinks I could have been working with someone." I glanced at Autumn. "Someone strong."

Her eyes widened. "Me?"

I understood how she could have thought that, and that was entirely my fault. I gave a vigorous shake of my head. "No, someone from the parkour class. He says I could have poisoned the dacquoise and then someone could have helped me move the body. What motivation they would have to help me with that kind of thing, I have no idea, but there you go. And there are plenty of strong, athletic people in that class. Eliza, David, Peter, Isaac—and Isaac found the body, so I'm assuming that's going to cause some trouble for him." I paused. "I just remembered that the sheriff doesn't know Isaac is in the class. He's focusing on the coaches. Well, that's good luck. We need to be careful not to let that slip."

Autumn's face had paled, and she moved toward the front door. "At the boardwalk, when the sheriff was talking with David, I thought that was the sheriff's regular routine. I didn't think he was actually serious about all that. Parkour people—they're a different breed. They're all about respect and discipline, and to them, the point of strength is so you can help people. They aren't murderers. I need to warn Peter and Eliza. And David. I'll warn the whole class, if it comes down to it."

"You could just call," Dottie said.

Autumn paused, the door partially open. "I better do this in person."

And then she disappeared, Skittles shooting past Autumn just before the door closed.

"That cat is going to think it can sneak through one of these days and won't make it," Dottie said. She was talking about the cat, but her thoughts seemed to be on something else entirely.

"What's on your mind?" I asked, packing up a box for the sheriff and Randy.

Dottie hesitated. "I'm probably making something out of nothing, but doesn't it strike you as strange that Autumn needed to go visit the coaches personally? A few phone calls would have done it. Or just call one of the coaches and let them disseminate the information. What is she going to do, visit all fifteen people who attend class individually?"

That was a good question.

"We aren't going to discover the answer while sitting in an empty bakery," I said, turning off the OPEN sign. "Is everything out of the oven?"

Dottie nodded. "Autumn finished up a couple hours ago."

"Perfect." I grabbed the sheriff's pastries, certain we'd run into him while we were out, probably at the most inopportune time, knowing my luck. When Dottie didn't immediately join me, I said, "There's only one way we're going to find out what's going on with that parkour class, and that's to follow Autumn. So, come on."

Dottie looked out through the large front windows. "I know I was the one who thought she might be up to something, but it feels wrong, sneaking around like that. If she sees us, she'll think we don't trust her."

I smiled and shook my head. "I'm glad I don't live in that head of yours. You're always in conflict with yourself —letter of the law versus spirit of the law. Rule follower versus empathetic human. But rest assured, we aren't following her because we don't trust her. We're following her so that innocent people aren't sent to prison for something they didn't do. What we're after is the truth. I know I made it sound like my stint in the big house was more akin to a vacation, but it wasn't nearly as nice as all that—just making the best of a bad situation."

Dottie smiled. "The big house?"

I tilted my head to the side. "Isn't that what people call it?"

"Not the people I talk to."

I pushed open the bakery door. "Regardless, we better hurry. I don't have the faintest idea where any of these people live."

Of course, we'd spent so much time debating the morality of following Autumn that by the time we'd gone outside, she was long gone. Even if we'd left at the same time as her, it had been blind optimism to think we'd actually be able to keep up.

"So, what now?" Dottie asked, her gaze sweeping the road in front of the bakery.

What now, indeed.

"I'm inclined to believe Autumn that those folks are a different kind of people," I said. "That means we need additional suspects. Telling the sheriff that I didn't do it isn't enough."

Dottie's entire demeanor slumped, and she looked like

she needed a chair. I hadn't realized just how much my arrest had taken out of her.

"Clarissa hasn't been examined yet," I offered, my gaze mirroring Dottie's, as if the answers were going to appear in front of us. "The sheriff hasn't mentioned her—no one has, except Isaac. I don't remember seeing her at the grand opening, and she certainly isn't strong enough to have carried a dead body. But she also has some really deep-seated rage. I know you were afraid of scaring her off, but maybe we could stop by for a neighborly chat."

Dottie gave me a sad smile. "We've never even spoken to her before, and now we're going to stop by her house? We won't make it past the front door."

"Yes, we will." I held up the pastry box. "No one can turn away free pastries. We'll get information and a new customer at the same time. I can make the sheriff another box when we get back."

"I'm impressed," Dottie said, and she looked it too. It wasn't easy to impress Dottie. "So, where does she live?"

That was a very good question and one I hadn't yet gotten the answer to. I hurried back inside and called Jessie from the store's phone.

When she answered, I could hear people in the background. Sounded like she was outside somewhere.

"Jessie, where does Clarissa live? We have some pastries for her."

"Really close to your store," Jessie half-shouted. Where

was she? "Halfway up your street on the left. 3422 is written on the mailbox."

"Thank you," I said, scribbling the numbers down on a pad of paper I kept next to the phone. Another shout from the background. Okay, I had to know where she was. There was nowhere in Starlight Ridge that had that many people gathered at one time, except maybe bingo. "What's all that noise?"

"Caleb let me borrow his car to go into the city. All I wanted was a new blouse but apparently there's a music festival going on. Appreciate the quiet while you can."

And then she hung up.

Well, alrighty then.

While I was here, I might as well use the bathroom. Just in case. I hated using other people's bathrooms, and I had no idea how long we'd be gone.

As soon as I re-exited the store, Dottie was leaning against the wall. "Emergency bathroom visit?"

"I don't use the bathroom every time I go inside."

She glanced at me. "I can smell the soap."

Darn Dottie and her highly tuned perceptive skills.

I didn't answer her but held up the piece of paper. "Got Clarissa's address."

Dottie moved to stand up, but just as she was reaching for her cane, Skittles ran past her and knocked over the cane, startling us both.

"I thought we'd decided we're going to retrain her to be an inside cat after we caught her going to the bathroom at the sunset stroll last week," Dottie said, even as she smiled at Skittles, who had returned and was rubbing against her leg. "We can't turn the beach into her own personal, and gigantic, litter box."

"I know, but it's easier said than done," I said. "It's not like either of us have the energy to chase after her." I moved to take the cat, but Skittles looked so happy with Dottie, like all she wanted was some love. She probably got lonely being cooped up all day, and I couldn't bring myself to lock her back up. I did pick her up, but I didn't return her inside. Instead, once Dottie was steady on her feet, cane in hand, I handed her the pastry box, and I nestled Skittles in my arms.

Dottie raised an eyebrow.

"What? She could use the fresh air. Besides, she'll help win Clarissa over. Everyone loves Skittles."

That was sometimes true. The other truth was that Skittles was a bit too curious for her own good and was as likely to cause trouble as she was to win them over. But seeing that she seemed to be in a cuddly and affectionate mood, it could only help our cause and give us a natural talking point.

Dottie looked skeptical, but then she raised a shoulder. "If you think so, but I can't carry the pastry box and use my cane at the same time. We should probably take my car."

"It's only a few houses down," I protested. "The exercise will do us some good, and we'll take it slow, I promise."

Dottie grumbled something about exercise being overrated but began the trek up the street. I kept glancing at the note in my hand, as if I were going to forget the house numbers. We'd made it to 3418 when someone emerged from a house two doors up. That had to be it.

But it wasn't Clarissa who exited the house.

It was Autumn.

16

Dottie and I both stopped mid-step, and I petted Skittles to keep her content while we waited to see what Autumn would do next. It wasn't like Dottie and I could hide, so if Autumn turned in our direction, she would know that she'd been spotted.

She didn't turn our way, though, instead heading up the street, eventually turning left at the corner.

Dottie and I released a collective sigh.

"Why did I feel like we needed to hide from her?" I asked as we resumed our walk. "We're supposed to be a team, and our bakery isn't going to be very successful if we're keeping secrets from each other."

"We're not the ones hiding things," Dottie said. "Autumn said she was going to visit the parkour coaches to warn them, and yet she's just up the road at Clarissa's house. She lied to us."

Yes, it did seem that way. But there had to be a logical explanation for it all.

"I suppose we better find out why, then," I said, quickening my pace, but then I slowed back down when I realized Dottie might have felt the same urgency I did, but she wasn't going to walk any faster than she already was.

When we arrived at 3422, I stared at the front door for longer than necessary, second-guessing what we were about to do. This was a woman who had the potential to lose her temper in a big way, and I didn't think I could handle being on the receiving end of that. She'd threatened to a kill a woman. Of course, we all threaten to kill someone at some point in our lives. But this time, a woman really had ended up dead. And we were about to walk into the potential suspect's living room and offer her pastries and a chance to pet our cat.

Dottie didn't feel the same trepidation I did, though, or at least didn't show it, and walked right up to the front door. She glanced back. "Well, come on." And then she rang the doorbell.

I joined her just as Clarissa opened the door.

She was a tall woman—much taller than she appeared in church. Must be long legs. Her hair was cut short, and she wore pajamas and a robe. Had we arrived too early in the day?

I glanced at my watch. No, it was two o'clock in the afternoon.

"Hello, Clarissa," Dottie said, her voice filled with

warmth. Wow, she never used that voice with me. "My name is Dorothy, and this is my sister, Josephine."

"But everyone calls me Jo," I interjected.

Dottie nodded but looked like she was suppressing an eye roll. "Yes, and we just opened the bakery at the bottom of the street."

Clarissa gave a curt nod. "Yes, I know who you are. Autumn is a friend of mine. Sorry I didn't make it to your grand opening. It's been busy around here."

Judging by the pajamas, I didn't know how true that was.

"You know Autumn?" Dottie asked, sounding genuinely surprised. I was too. It turned out Autumn was full of surprises, and not the good kind.

Clarissa nodded again. "Yes. Known her for years. She went to high school with my son."

Relief coursed through me. Of course they'd know each other. They'd both lived in Starlight Ridge, where everyone knows everyone. After a year, Dottie and I knew a lot of people, but we still hadn't mastered the entire town directory.

"I can't think of a better person than Autumn," Dottie said. "We're lucky to have her at the bakery." She then held up the box of pastries. "We see you in church every week and thought we'd bring some pastries for you to try, since you haven't yet had the chance. We're always asking ourselves, what would Jesus do? And it turns out, he would bring you pastries." Clarissa's eyes lit up until Dottie added, "Would you mind if we came in?"

Clarissa's guard immediately rose, and she eyed us like we were door to door salesmen. She didn't want to say yes, but she also didn't want to say no to free pastries.

"I'm sorry, I don't think so," she said, making up her mind and starting to close the door. "Maybe next time." The way she was positioning her body, it was as if she didn't want us to see something behind her, and I doubted there would be a next time.

"Maybe we can just leave them with you, then," Dottie said, extending the box toward her. At this point, I didn't think it had anything to do with questioning Clarissa or gaining a new customer. From the way Dottie was trying to get rid of that box, her arms were tired.

Clarissa hesitated, but how could she turn down an offer like that? She gave us a small smile. "Thank you."

As she reached for the box, Skittles must have seen something that interested her because she leaped from my arms and raced past Clarissa into the house.

She gave a small scream. "Oh, no. That cat can't be in my house." She looked at us with horror. "I'm allergic."

Allergic to cats. Of course. That was why Clarissa hadn't invited us inside, and now we were going to inadvertently kill her. It seemed prison was destined to be a part of my future, one way or another.

"I'll get her," I said, rushing past Clarissa before she had the chance to say no. Dottie wasn't going to be any help with chasing Skittles, and I'd perfected the ancient art of luring her with treats. I'd brought some in my pocket, just in case. Deep down, I must have known something like this was going to happen.

"Skittles," I said, clicking my tongue. "I have treats."

Had calling a cat ever worked in the history of luring cats? No. But I had to at least sound like I was trying while I figured out where the heck that feline had run off to.

The problem was that the house was a mess. A hoarder's dream and everyone else's nightmare. Random objects cluttered every part of every room. Tables were filled with boxes, old pictures, and dirty dishes.

Skittles could be hiding anywhere.

A small and dusty surfboard sat in the corner and would be the perfect shield. I peeked behind it. Nope.

What was an old tire doing shoved under the kitchen table? It seemed like a lovely place for a cat to curl up, and I bent over the best I could to look inside. Alas, a circular wooden board had been bolted over the tire's hole. That was when I heard the crash from the cabinets behind me in the kitchen. I hurried over, Clarissa chasing after me now that she'd recovered from her shock, telling me that she'd retrieve the cat and asking me to stay with Dottie.

"Nonsense. You're allergic, you shouldn't be touching the cat," I said. One of the lower cabinets had been left open, and I saw movement inside. It was one of those lazy Susans, where you could spin the shelf inside to access whatever you needed. I'd always felt sorry for the bad rap the Susans of the world had received, now forever associated with laziness. I felt especially sorry for the one Susan the invention was named after. Probably the inventor's ex-wife. A final dig that had followed her everywhere.

There behind all the canned tomatoes was Skittles, exploring her own little cave.

"Skittles, I have your treats," I said, placing several on a can in front of her. She ate them. I then placed more on the next can closer to me. Gradually, she moved close enough that I could pick her up. I held her close, not giving her the opportunity for a second escape attempt. "That was a naughty thing you did," I told her, and then realized I had just rewarded her for the behavior with half a bag of treats.

A few cans had been knocked over, and I spun the shelf so I could right them. Upon fixing the last can, I noticed a small container stuck in a back corner. It was similar to what I would get from the pharmacy, except the label had been torn off.

Clarissa charged up behind me, freaking out that I needed to get out of her house.

I apologized profusely for Skittles' behavior and hurried out before anything could be thrown at me like she'd done with Florence.

Once Skittles and I were outside and the front door had been properly slammed in my face, I bent over, the stress of the event weighing heavily as my heart raced.

"That went well," Dottie said dryly. I noticed she was

box-free, so Clarissa had kept the pastries. "Maybe you'll agree now that Skittles should be an inside cat."

I nodded, sucking in a lungful of the salty air. "Yes, that might be wise. I hate the thought of trapping her inside the bakery, but we'll have enough customers that she'll get plenty of social interaction."

"Do we have any other customers who are allergic to cats? We might need to keep Skittles up in the apartment during the day." Dottie sounded sad at the prospect, and I mirrored those feelings.

"If Skittles' presence keeps at least Clarissa away from the bakery, the cat's worth keeping around the store. I don't think I could handle another encounter with her for a while. In fact, it might be good to skip church altogether for a couple of weeks. Until we hear that the town council has appointed a new bingo caller, anyway. Hopefully they'll still be using the extra card as a bribe for church attendance. Not that I need the additional luck, but it never hurts."

Dottie smirked as we walked back to the bakery. "I guess that was a bust, huh?"

"Yeah. Even if we had been invited in, there was no way we'd find anything. I don't know if that show *Hoarders* is still on TV. But if it is, we need to give them a call. That place is insane."

"Maybe they'd find a murder weapon," Dottie said with a little laugh. "That would be an iconic episode, huh?"

I laughed. "If only."

17

Pounding on the apartment door. An incessant ringing of the doorbell.

It was eight o'clock in the evening, and I had just been getting ready for bed.

Dottie stuck her head out of her bedroom, curlers in her hair. "Who could that be at this hour?"

I tossed a worried look toward the door. "It sounds like it could be an emergency." Wrapping my robe around me, I hurried across the apartment and opened the door.

I should have used the peephole first.

Sheriff Hart pushed past me into the apartment without even a hello.

"I didn't invite you in, sheriff," I said. "You know that visits are limited to business hours. Come back tomorrow."

He held up a piece of paper, as if that should be answer enough.

"I don't know what that is." Exasperation and exhaustion tinged my voice. All I wanted in life right now was to read a nice book for a few minutes in bed before falling asleep. Was that too much to ask?

"It's a search warrant," he said.

For once, my words failed me. "A search—what on earth for?"

Sheriff Hart didn't answer me, instead starting with the kitchen, opening and closing cupboards and drawers as if he owned the place.

Randy showed up at the same time Dottie exited her room. Her eyes held fire. Randy's gaze dropped, and he mumbled some apologies before joining the sheriff.

"They have a search warrant," I told her before she ended up doing something that would get us into further trouble. "Do they have to tell us why?"

Dottie's gaze followed the sheriff and Randy as they moved into our small living room. "No, they don't."

I nodded, watching them work. "Is this routine for a murder investigation?"

Even as I said it, I knew it wasn't. Even when all signs had pointed to me and Sheriff Hart had taken me in, it hadn't felt serious. No one had stormed our apartment. It had been more like make-believe—like the sheriff had been going through the motions because he was supposed to, but it was without any real conviction.

Even with all these theatrics, though, I wasn't worried. They weren't going to find anything.

Until they did.

"Sheriff Hart," Randy called from my bedroom. "I have an unmarked prescription bottle."

The sheriff speed walked from Dottie's room into mine. "Where was it?"

"Jacket pocket."

"Bag it. We'll have them open it in the lab. If that's what we're looking for, we don't want to be messing with that stuff."

My gaze snapped to Dottie, my heart racing. I was having trouble breathing, having to pull air in through gasps. "I didn't kill Florence," I said, feeling woozy.

Dottie's eyes held a sadness I'd never seen. Like it didn't matter if I had or not—she couldn't help me now.

And then everything went black.

MY EYES BLINKED OPEN, my head pounding. I reached for the glass of water I always kept at the side of my bed, but my hand jerked back halfway to the nightstand.

I blinked a couple more times, the room starting to come into focus.

This wasn't my bedroom, and there was a pink hospital thermos with a straw sticking out of it on the table next to me. I tried to reach it, but once again, something was holding me back.

Handcuffs. Just on the one wrist.

"I'll move it to the other wrist. I didn't realize you

wouldn't be able to reach your water," Sheriff Hart said from the other side of the room.

I started, having thought I was alone. He stood and stretched his arms high over his head, as if he'd been in that chair for a long time.

"What happened?" I asked, using my free hand to brush my fingers through my hair. It was a mess, I was sure. I wondered if they'd allow me a brush. Just because I was in the hospital didn't mean I had to completely let myself go. Even in this humiliating hospital gown, I still had some self-respect.

"We found the murder weapon in your jacket pocket," he said, unlocking the handcuffs, then moving the cuff to my other wrist. It clicked shut. This was it. They were going to transfer me to one of the big prisons—the type that don't bring in mattresses and decent food. From now on, it was cots and oatmeal. I supposed I'd need to join a gang once I got in there—get me some protection.

"I found it," I said. "In Clarissa's kitchen."

Sheriff Hart didn't seem at all surprised, which meant that Dottie had already tried explaining what had happened. "If that were true, you'd have called me to come retrieve it—not taken it yourself, risking further incrimination. Dottie would never have allowed something like that."

"She didn't know I'd found it."

The sheriff nodded. "Yes, she told me about your... problem. Awfully convenient that you just so happen to be a kleptomaniac who doesn't have control when she takes things."

I lifted the hand that was handcuffed. "I assure you, Sheriff, it is far from convenient." My gaze landed on the window. It wasn't much of a view—nothing like Starlight Ridge. I couldn't see anything except the roof of the hospital. "I've tried to get help. Even saw a therapist for a while. He tried to go back to my childhood—figure out when it all started. The only thing I learned was that even though I had loving parents, somehow this was their fault. I stopped going."

Sheriff Hart nodded, trying to be polite but obviously not believing a word I was saying. "You passed out when we found the weapon," he said. "You have some pretty nasty bruises, and you hit your head hard—that's why we brought you into the main hospital. Your little clinic wasn't going to cut it this time. Once you're discharged, you'll be transferred to the prison here in the city, where you'll await trial."

"I didn't do it," I said. "The reason you released me in the first place was because you believed it was impossible for me to have committed the crime, at least alone, and if I have to prove it, I will. Tell me how much bail is, and I'll get the money. I'll—"

"There is no bail," Sheriff Hart interrupted. "You are a murder suspect. I released you because I couldn't tie you to the murder weapon—not because I thought it impossible that you were involved. And now we've found the murder weapon in your bedroom. In your jacket pocket."

For a moment there, I'd thought we could talk through this misunderstanding. That he'd see it was silly to think me capable of something like this.

The time for talking was past.

"Who was my accomplice, then?" I asked.

Sheriff Hart quieted as he considered me. "I was hoping that was something you'd be willing to share with me. Maybe we can work out a deal if you tell me who the brains behind the murder was."

"Brains?" I said, my voice squawking as it went three octaves too high. "You don't think I'm smart enough to pull off something like this?"

As soon as I said it, I knew it had been a mistake. He'd been goading me—using my pride against me. And it had worked. Except, I hadn't actually committed the crime, and I'd just made it sound as if I had.

"Maybe it was Clarissa," he said. "That could be why you told me you'd found the poison in her home. Throwing her under the bus, as it were."

I pulled in a deep breath, attempting to keep my anger in check.

"I did not have an accomplice, because I didn't do it," I said. "And I really did find the poison in Clarissa's kitchen in her lazy Susan. Behind the canned tomatoes. Of course, I didn't mean to take it with me. Dottie usually checks my pockets when I leave places, but Clarissa wasn't happy with me snooping around, and we needed to leave as quickly as possible. I wonder if she'd hidden it there after—"

I was about to voice out loud that Clarissa could have hidden the cyanide after Autumn stopped by. Maybe Autumn had said something that made Clarissa antsy. But then that would have thrown our pastry chef in the sheriff's crosshairs for a second time, and we really did rely on her to keep the bakery open. Even if I was locked up, the bakery could live on. Dottie and Autumn would be sad at first, of course, but they'd adapt and learn to move on.

"After what?" Sheriff Hart said, walking closer. "What aren't you telling me?"

I held up a finger, asking for a moment to think. Autumn had been going to warn the parkour coaches that the sheriff was interested in them and to be careful. She had gone to Clarissa's house instead. Had that been to warn her as well?

But Autumn couldn't be involved in this. No way. I wouldn't even entertain the thought.

"Clarissa hid the poison after she heard us coming," I finished. "We'd brought Skittles with us, which I will admit was a mistake. Skittles got loose. That's why we were in the house in the first place, because Skittles had gotten bored at the bakery, and Clarissa's home certainly has plenty to explore." When the sheriff gave me a blank look, I said, "She has a hoarding problem."

Realization struck me. "You haven't been inside her

house. Which means that even after Dottie told you that was where I'd found the poison, you didn't follow up on that line of investigation. You've already determined that I'm guilty."

Sheriff Hart held up a finger and began ticking off reasons he believed I was guilty. "One, you were the person who packaged and sold the pastry to Florence." He held up a second finger. "Two, you were the only one behind the counter, so no one would have seen you amid the chaos. Three, you have motive. Florence berated your chef and her pastries in front of everyone, and if she had continued to do so, and if people believed her, that could have meant closing down your bakery." He held up a fourth finger. "Four, the murder weapon was discovered in your bedroom."

I felt like there should be a fifth reason to even things out—that was the OCD part of me. Maybe it was klepto-mania's cousin that liked to hang out.

But then I realized something. My gaze snapped up. "Who called you?"

The sheriff paused and gave me a curious look. "Sorry?"

"Someone tipped you off that I had the murder weapon. They had to have known I had taken it. How, unless they were in fact the murderer and wanted to frame me? So I'm going to ask again—who called you?"

Sheriff Hart looked uncomfortable, like he didn't appreciate that I was now the one asking questions—and very good ones, if I said so myself. "It was an anonymous caller. But we get those all the time. You don't want it to get out that you were the one who called the cops on the sweet old lady down at the bakery. And if that sweet old lady really was the murderer, you certainly wouldn't want her sister to be out for vengeance."

I understood that, because, in all likelihood, that would be the scenario.

However, I didn't think that was what was happening here.

"They called your cell phone, right?"

The sheriff gave a small nod.

"So, you can trace the phone number. Or better yet, talk to Jessie. She'll know whose number that was. If it's some random person in town, fine. Don't do anything about it. But if it's Clarissa's—"

"I still wouldn't tell you," the sheriff interrupted. He turned toward the door, then glanced back. "I'm going to check in with the doctor and let him know you're awake. If you need anything, you have the nurse's button."

And then he left.

I'd gotten under his skin, I knew it.

And when he discovered that the anonymous caller was in fact Clarissa, a woman who had made a desperate phone call because she had found her bottle of cyanide missing, he'd have no choice but to let me go.

I was sure of it.

18

I didn't think people were supposed to know where I was, but that hadn't stopped Dottie from calling my room. And because the sheriff had left, there was nothing he could do about it. He'd been gone much longer than anticipated—certainly longer than it would take to talk to the doctor—and I hoped that meant he was taking my questions seriously.

"How are you doing?" Dottie asked. "Just another spa day filled with *Ted Lasso*, I'm sure."

I hesitated, wondering how much to tell her. She'd freak out if I told her what kind of real trouble I was in. Maybe it was better that she not know—I didn't think her heart could take much more than it already had.

"Just another spa day," I said. "No *Ted Lasso*, but they're feeding me well. I'm embarrassed that I passed out the way I did."

Dottie laughed. "Don't pretend you didn't plan it that way. It was genius. Much better to be at the hospital than booked at the local jail. He can't do much with you while you're there."

Even though my sister acted like everything was fine and this was just another one of my adventures, I could hear the worry in her voice. She knew that me passing out hadn't been planned. And she must have known I was in more trouble than I was letting on.

"Can I ask you a favor?" I asked.

"Anything," Dottie said.

"The sheriff said he received an anonymous call that I had the cyanide. The only one who could have known that was the murderer. And since I took it from Clarissa's kitchen—"

"She must be the anonymous caller," Dottie finished for me. "So, what do you need me to do?"

I had been going to ask Dottie to get proof, but then what? Even if Clarissa was the anonymous caller, how would she have killed Florence? She had been one of the few people who hadn't attended the grand opening, and she certainly wasn't strong enough to carry Florence's body all the way from her home to the beach, unless she was much stronger than she appeared.

"I don't know," I said, releasing a dejected sigh. "Clarissa did it. I'm sure of it. She had the motive, but not the opportunity. And we don't have any proof. Because I stole it."

This mess that I was in—it was my fault. I had tried to get help with my condition in the past, but I must not have worked hard enough. Hadn't put in enough effort. Otherwise, I would have cured myself and we wouldn't be in this situation.

Dottie got quiet for a minute. "It's not your fault. The doctor went over this. It has to do with an imbalance of the chemicals in your brain. Mom had it too, and she didn't put nearly the amount of effort into getting better that you have. You always make sure to return whatever you steal and make amends. You don't deserve to be in prison for it, and you certainly don't deserve to be accused of murder. When I decided to become a cop—"

"It was because of how I was treated when we were teenagers," I finished. "But this isn't a robe from a hotel or a tin of candies from a friend's house. I stole evidence. Something that could have proven that Clarissa did it."

"Except that the sheriff would never have gotten a search warrant for her home. There was no need. In his eyes, everyone in town had the motive, so he was focusing on the opportunity and the ability—which was exactly what he should have done."

I rubbed an eyebrow. "But I couldn't have moved the body. I don't have the ability."

Silence.

"Jo, this has nothing to do with moving the body. She was dead before everything was staged."

What my sister was saying was that the moving of the

body was a moot point. This had to do with the murder, not an accomplice who had been trying to help me cover it up. It didn't matter if I couldn't have lifted the body.

"Is there anything left to do, then?" I asked. "Surely the sheriff will try to pull prints off the medicine bottle. Maybe I'll get lucky and Clarissa's will be on there."

"Maybe," Dottie said. "So, then they arrest you both. Now they have your accomplice."

I snorted. "Yeah, I'd like to see Clarissa try to lift anything other than that..." I stopped. Clarissa was a hoarder, and her home was a kleptomaniac's dream. I could steal an item a day for a year and she'd never notice. But not all of the items in her home were hers.

"Surfboard," I said. "And a tire. It had a circular piece of wood in the middle where the hole usually is."

"O-kay," Dottie said slowly. "What of it? There were all sorts of random things in her house. I only peeked in through the front door and felt overwhelmed by the clutter."

I was getting excited now. Yes, I could see how she could have pulled it off. But how to get the sheriff to believe me enough to drive me back to Starlight Ridge?

"Dottie, you love me, right?"

A pause. It was too long for my liking, and I could practically hear the wheels in her mind spinning, wondering why I was asking.

She gave a hesitant "Yes."

"I need you to call the sheriff and tell him you found something strange at the bakery and that he ought to take a look. And that he should bring me along."

"You want me to make a false report."

I shook my head, forgetting she couldn't see me. "No, not false. By the time he gets there, it will be very real."

"If I ask him to bring you, he'll see right through it," Dottie said.

That was true.

What to do—

The hospital room door opened, and Sheriff Hart strode in. He stopped when he saw that I was on the phone. Red moved up his neck, and he turned and barked into the hallway, "I asked that that phone be removed."

He then turned back to me and waited for an explanation.

That was when I turned on the waterworks and with a shaky voice said into the phone, "Thank you for letting me know. We'll leave right away. Please ask her to meet me at the bakery in a couple of hours. She needs to know that I'm taking care of everything."

And then I hung up on Dottie, hoping all those years on the force would help her understand the cryptic message.

"It's just awful," I told the sheriff, tears streaming down my cheeks. I was grateful for all those community plays I'd been in as a teenager. "The murderer. They've struck again. If we don't hurry—well, we might already be too late."

The sheriff's face slackened. "You can't be serious."

I gave a timid nod and then buried my face in my hands, purposely poking myself in the eye as I did so. I had intended for it to make my crying more believable, but I poked my eye too hard, resulting in real tears. I held out a hand. "Tissue," I whimpered.

"People should be calling me, not the woman in the hospital," he grumbled as he grabbed the tissue box off the side table. He glanced at me. "I can't take you back to Starlight Ridge. You haven't been discharged from the hospital, and I told the prison I'd be bringing you in as soon as—"

That made me fake-cry harder. "Don't you see that it couldn't have been me?" I gulped in air as I tried to breathe, and the sheriff waved a hand in the air, seemingly trying to make the waterworks stop.

"Yes, yes, and if what you're saying is true... I'll talk to the doctor." Sheriff Hart ran from the room, his expression panicked.

I felt bad for misleading the sheriff. I'd made sure to never lie, though. I may have said just enough to give a false impression, but I'd never lied. The most important thing was to get me back to Starlight Ridge. The murderer would likely not hurt anyone else—they didn't have the need. But they were more than willing to let an old lady take the fall for their actions—even go to prison for the rest of my life—and I was not okay with the type of person who would do that.

The end justified the means.

Ten minutes later, the sheriff returned, handcuff keys in hand. "All of your lab work came back fine, so I've signed all the paperwork to get you out of here," he said. "But you are still under arrest for Florence's murder. That means I'm going to treat you as such. Back of the car, where you can't stab me, handcuffs—everything. This is not a joy ride."

Funny how quickly he had gone from a sheriff who was going through the motions to a real cop who wasn't going to take any nonsense from me. I missed the old Sheriff Hart, but I couldn't imagine the tremendous pressure he must be under.

"I appreciate you doing a thorough job," I told him. "You are a gem, Sheriff Hart. You are doing beautifully for your first murder investigation, and I'll be sure to tell your boss exactly that. Do you have a boss?"

Sheriff Hart paused, as if trying to figure out my game. "I don't. All decisions start and end with me. But," he eyed me warily, "thank you for understanding the difficult position I am in. I didn't want to have to arrest you, Jo. I don't like seeing you like this. But I have to follow the evidence. Even good people do terrible things sometimes."

Dottie had said the same thing. "I do understand that," I said. "And it led you to me. But now we have bigger problems at hand. I'll sit in the back of the car, handcuffed, if that makes you feel better, but we need to get back to Starlight Ridge right away. As the saying goes, the mice will play when the..." I paused, waiting for him to finish my sentence.

"When the cat is away," he said, his expression softening.

19

The sheriff's car lumbered to a slow stop in front of the bakery. I looked for movement inside but didn't see anything. The sign in the front window said CLOSED, and I wondered if it had said that since I'd been taken to the hospital. I hoped not. Dottie needed something, other than worry, to keep her mind busy.

"No one has called me," the sheriff said, opening the back door. "If this is some elaborate escape plan—"

Dottie didn't give him time to finish. She opened the front door, shouting, "Jo, hurry. She'll be here any minute," and then gestured for me to follow her.

"It's not, I assure you," I said, feeling guilty for his shocked expression at seeing Dottie alive and well. I didn't feel guilty enough to not hurry after Dottie, my hands awkwardly handcuffed behind my back as I entered the shop.

Dottie locked the front door behind me. "I thought about telling her to meet us at the apartment, but it's too confined. No good exits except the main door." She herded me toward the back. "A good meet-up location has a few exit strategies. We only have two here, but at least we won't have to deal with stairs."

Sheriff Hart was now at the front door, shouting, though his words were muffled. There was even some pounding involved. I wondered how long we had until he decided to break the glass.

"What are we going to do about the sheriff?" I asked. "As soon as she sees him, she'll be scared off, thinking this is a trap."

Dottie smiled. "I thought of that. I told her that the sheriff was staking out the front so to enter through the kitchen entrance and we'd meet in there. I said that if she made one wrong move, we'd walk right out and feed our new evidence to the sheriff."

I cocked an eyebrow. "Why would she agree to come at all, then, knowing the sheriff is right outside?"

"Because I don't want to give the evidence to the sheriff. I want money for my silence."

Oh. That was devious. I hadn't realized that Dottie had it in her. "I take it she doesn't know I'm here. That she thinks you're the type of sister who would sell my soul in exchange for a few bucks."

Dottie nodded. "Yup."

For someone who never stepped their toe over the line,

Dottie was much too good at arranging clandestine meetups. It made me wonder what she'd been asked to do as a cop in the name of the law.

She looked like she was about to say more, but paused and raised a finger to her lips. "I heard something back there. Let's go."

We went through the Employees Only door and entered the kitchen.

I worried about the locked front door—we weren't only keeping the sheriff out but were also locking ourselves in. And we might need the sheriff if things got dicey. I hadn't told Dottie everything I'd realized—hadn't had the time. If it was just Clarissa we'd be dealing with, the sheriff's absence wouldn't be a big deal.

Hopefully he'd break in sooner than later.

There was no time to explain this to Dottie, however, because the back door opened and in walked...

"Peter," Dottie said, her lips parting in surprise as her gaze whipped to me. He was wearing a leather jacket, his hair pulled back in one of his bandanas. One hand was shoved in his pocket, and the other held a box from our bakery. Likely the same one we'd delivered to his mother the previous day.

"It was Clarissa I invited to the shop." Dottie turned back to Peter, her eyes narrowing. "I won't negotiate with you."

I readjusted my hands, making them as small as possible, and wiggled out of the handcuffs. The shrinking that comes with age had finally come in handy. The cuffs fell to the floor with a clatter, and I massaged my wrists. Much better.

"It was never Clarissa," I said. "She wasn't at the grand opening. But he was. And he's strong enough to move a body."

Dottie looked like she was having a difficult time wrapping her head around what I was saying. "So, Clarissa asked Peter to do it for her? That doesn't make sense. He had no motive to help her with something like that."

I turned to Peter. "She knew what you'd done, and she covered for you, but she never asked you to poison Florence, did she?"

Peter's eyes hardened, his body taut, like he was ready to make a run for it. "She didn't have the guts. Florence had never had to deal with the consequences of killing my brother, and yet she was the one flinging undeserved abuse at my mom. And my mom just stood by and took it. Sure, she threw a tantrum once in a while. All the grief and pain exploding out, but never in ways that mattered."

"Mom?" Dottie mouthed.

I nodded and pointed to Peter. "When Autumn left us to warn the parkour coaches, her first stop was at Clarissa's house. We thought it was because Autumn might be involved, but she wasn't there to visit Clarissa—it was Peter she went to see."

Peter's gaze dropped. "I never meant to get Autumn into trouble. I'd hoped the sheriff wouldn't look further than the knife wound. It wasn't like we are known for our amazing law enforcement out here. No need for a toxicology report when Florence had obviously been stabbed."

"You didn't drag Florence down to the beach in her scuba gear because you cared about Autumn," I said with a sad shake of my head. "You knew someone was going to have to take the blame for her death. You were just trying to ensure it wasn't you. And the less the situation resembled what really happened, the better. You poisoned the dacquoise while at our bakery, right?"

After a brief hesitation, Peter nodded. "Florence had just purchased her pastries and you were helping the next customer. She'd placed the box on the counter while returning her wallet to her purse. I took advantage of her distraction to open the box and administer the cyanide. She caught me closing the lid and I was afraid she's seen the poison, but she thought I was trying to steal one of her desserts. I pretended that I had been. She said a few unkind words and then left in a huff." He didn't look happy about how the events had transpired and he released a long sigh.

"Even though I'd been in procession of the cyanide for several months, I hadn't determined how I was going to do it until I heard about your grand opening. The whole town in one place like that—it was what I needed. Even though there would be some communal desserts, it was likely that Florence would purchase some to take home. Naturally, I didn't want to accidentally poison the wrong person."

"How kind of you," I said, dryly.

Peter didn't pay me any attention. It seemed this confession was cathartic for him and he continued. "I hadn't planned on the scuba gear. I knew the police would start their investigation with the party's guests. Including me. And yes, also the bakery's employees. But I'd thought with so many potential suspects and so many with motive, the police would never be able to figure it out. But then—" Peter's voice hitched. "When I left the bakery, I started analyzing all the possible scenarios and I realized I had made a mistake. It likely wouldn't be too difficult for the sheriff to figure out if someone had purchased cyanide, leading them to me. And even if the sheriff wasn't able to track down the poison, believe it or not, Autumn was also a factor in my decision. She was the one who had access to all the food—the one who had baked it all. The blame would fall on her—I really did want to keep her out of it. I knew I had to improvise."

Dottie looked disgusted. "Don't pretend you care about her. What you did—dressing up an old woman and stabbing her with her own knife, you did that because you were looking out for yourself. You didn't care where the blame landed, as long as it couldn't be traced back to you."

As miserable as Peter looked for what he'd done, I had to agree with my sister. "Did you mean for it to look like suicide?" I asked. "Is that why you planted the beer bottles to make it look like she'd been drinking?"

Peter's expression lightened and he laughed at that.

"Oh, no, those were mine. I had to be drunk to follow through with my plan, and I forgot they were there. Good thing the sheriff didn't gather them as evidence. My DNA would have been all over them. I went back and picked them up the following morning."

It was then that I remembered the beer bottle that Jessie had found in front of our store on the night of the grand opening. "The sheriff wasn't interested in the beer bottles," I grumbled. "Never stopped to think that they might be important."

Dottie frowned. "What I still don't understand is why." She paused. "Peter, you don't seem the type to do something like this. Autumn told us that you parkour folks are a different breed. Better than most. She was convinced it couldn't have been any of you."

"Autumn always did think the best of people," Peter said, his voice soft.

I rested a hand on Dottie's shoulder. "Remember, Florence had been babysitting Peter's younger brother when he drowned." I glanced at Peter. "The surfboard that's in the corner of your living room. It was smaller than most, and dusty. Was that his?"

Peter nodded. "Yes. He'd just started learning. He was at that stage where he had learned a little—just enough to think that he knew everything. He took that board out into the ocean while Florence sat inside reading a book. And she kept on reading, even as he got out too far to be able to come back on his own. She was the reason he died. The reason my parents got a divorce. And all this time, my mom has kept that damn surfboard—a constant reminder of a tragedy I've never been able to escape. But did it affect Florence's life at all?"

He released a humorless laugh. "She's been able to live her best life, not a care in the world. And then to make her the town's official bingo caller instead of my mom—oh, how Florence gloated over that. I couldn't take it anymore. The police had ruled my brother's death an accident, and she never paid for what she did. For what she put my family through."

I released a sad sigh. "Peter, you didn't need to punish her—she's been punishing herself every minute since that day. Why do you think she was so angry all the time and couldn't stop bragging about being the bingo caller? Because she had nothing else."

"She wasn't just punishing herself," Dottie grumbled. "She punished everyone else too."

I raised a shoulder in concession. "True."

Dottie nodded to Peter as she asked me, "How did you know that he was Clarissa's son?"

"I didn't at first. But there was something about that tire under the dining room table that was nagging at me. On the way here, I remembered. I'd seen it in parkour class. The advanced group was using it. And the only one who would have one of those would be an instructor. Peter also seemed about the right age—it was more conjecture than anything."

Dottie shook her head. "Jo, that's some shoddy police work. We don't accuse someone based on conjecture."

"I didn't accuse," I protested. "He's the one who showed up at the bakery, ready to pay us for our silence."

Peter placed the bakery box on the floor before pulling a flask out of his pocket. He took a long pull. "I was never going to pay," he said.

He was drinking, which meant that, just like with Florence, he was getting ready to do something he would never dare do sober.

Yes, there were two exits, but Dottie hadn't taken into account that it would be Peter instead of Clarissa. Which meant that he was faster than us. Stronger. And he was standing in front of the closest door. It was slightly ajar, which was helpful, but it didn't matter—we'd never make it past him. We'd need to somehow make our way to the front door and unlock it before he caught up with us.

Our chances weren't looking good.

Until Dottie pulled out her gun.

"This is a citizen's arrest. Put your hands up," she barked.

Oh, right. Dottie, as a former cop, would have a gun on her if she was planning on meeting with a murderer. She knew I hated guns, and she kept it locked in a safe most of the time. Thankfully, despite her diminishing health, her marksmanship hadn't suffered, and I hoped Peter didn't try to put it to the test.

Peter ignored the gun. Instead, he bent over and

opened the pastry box. He slowly picked up an éclair, examining it as if he'd never seen one before.

"I meant these for you two," he said, his focus still on the pastry. "Thought I'd leave the box here and claim my mother hadn't liked them. You two would have a snack—you couldn't resell these eclairs now—and that would be the end of your snooping where you don't belong." He paused. "I suppose it's better this way. Like Autumn, you're innocent and good. And there was always the chance she might have eaten one of these by accident." He glanced at me. "Take care of her, please. She doesn't have any family left."

"No," I yelled, realizing what he intended to do. I grabbed Dottie's cane from her, and she stumbled as I rushed forward. Just as Peter was about to take a bite, I used the cane to whack the éclair out of his hand. "That was a good éclair before you weaponized it. Shame on you."

And then I leaned on Dottie's cane, my breaths coming out in gasps. Confronting murderers—this was a young person's game.

Sheriff Hart burst through the back door at that moment, his gun already raised as he barked for Peter to get on the ground.

"Oh, thank goodness," Dottie said, her entire body crumbling to the floor. "I don't think I'd have been able to shoot that poor boy."

I walked slowly over to her and returned her cane, only turning back when Sheriff Hart called me.

"You're lucky he left the back door ajar and I overheard enough to know what was going on, otherwise it would have been you and Dottie I'd have been ordering on the ground," he said. He patted his belt. "I don't have a second pair of handcuffs. Where are the ones I put on you?"

I gave him a sheepish smile and picked them up from where they'd dropped on the floor. "I didn't like wearing them."

He gave me an incredulous look as I handed them to him. "You slipped out of them?"

"Age has its advantages."

Sheriff Hart used his key to unlock them and then handcuffed Peter. I didn't think Peter would have as easy a time with them as I had. I walked the two men through the kitchen and to the shop, where I unlocked the front door. The sheriff then put Peter in the back of the car—there would be no front seat privileges for him. This was the real deal.

I leaned against the front of the store—I couldn't wait until I could lie down.

"You put yourselves in a very dangerous situation," the sheriff said, slamming the car door and turning to me. "If I hadn't come around looking for a back door, you two could have easily ended up like Florence."

"Dottie had it covered. She's excellent with a gun," I

said, pretending the situation hadn't been as dangerous as the sheriff was trying to get me to believe.

But it had been.

I'd forgotten about Dottie's gun—an out of sight, out of mind kind of thing—and had gone in only armed with accusations. There had been no plan except to get him to confess.

And then what? March him out to the sheriff's car, proudly proclaiming we had a murderer, with only our word against Peter's?

I hadn't thought things through, and I'd nearly gotten us killed in the process.

The sheriff shook his head. "Please promise me that you'll never do anything like that again. I've said it before —I like you. And I prefer you two stay alive."

I smiled. "As do I. Good thing we won't have to worry about getting ourselves into this situation again. Starlight Ridge isn't the type of place where people end up dead. Usually."

Sheriff Hart opened his door. "I'd like to believe that." And then he slid into his seat, gave a little wave, and drove off with Peter.

"He's right, you know," Dottie said as soon as I reentered the bakery.

She sat on the stool behind the display counter. Exhaustion had taken over, and she'd placed her chin in her hands. It seemed that was the only thing keeping her upright.

"You took unnecessary risks," she said.

I straightened. "That's better than not taking risks at all. Where would we be if we hadn't visited Clarissa?"

"You wouldn't have been on your way to prison, for one."

That was a valid point, but not entirely accurate.

"The sheriff never would have found the cyanide without our intervention. He wasn't about to search Clarissa's house, and he'd certainly never have looked behind the canned tomatoes. And I would have still been arrested because I was the one with the opportunity."

Dottie nodded. "You can thank Skittles for that one."

Speaking of. I glanced around, the cat nowhere in sight. "Where is she? I hope you didn't trap her upstairs in the apartment. She needs at least a little bit of freedom, especially with how helpful she's been."

Helpful was the nice way of putting it, but it had all worked out in the end.

Before Dottie could answer, we heard a faint mew from behind me. I turned to see Skittles sitting on the sidewalk on the other side of the front door, asking to be let back in.

I grinned and opened the door. "Sorry, Dottie. There are just some people—and cats—that will always find a way around the rules."

"Don't I know it," Dottie said, pushing herself up to her feet. "And I'll figure out how to deal with you people—and cats—once I've had a nap. It's exhausting living with you two."

20

I practically skipped as we crossed the beach, Dottie and Autumn trying to keep up. Practically being the key word. I wasn't quite there yet, but give me enough time, and nothing would be able to slow me down.

"Are you sure you want to try this again?" Dottie said. "I thought we'd agreed that once was enough."

I paused and turned back. She had taken a break and was leaning on her cane, pulling in a deep breath. "Of course I'm not sure. But that's the point, isn't it? If we can solve two murders, surely we can do other unexpected things."

Dottie didn't look convinced.

I nodded toward her cane. "Do you realize that you've forgotten to use that thing at least three times in the past week? Because you were busy and focused on other things.

So, let's keep you busy and gain some muscle while we're at it."

Autumn grinned. "I like how you think." Her smile dipped. "It will be different without Peter, though. I can't believe he would do something like that." Her gaze met mine. "You should have called me."

I hesitated.

It hadn't been a lot, but it was enough to give her the general idea of why we hadn't called. Her lips parted in surprise. "You thought I was involved?"

"We didn't think you'd murdered anyone," Dottie said quickly. "But we did see you come out of Clarissa's house right before we found the poison in her cupboard. And we didn't know what that meant."

"You thought that maybe I knew who had done it and I was trying to protect them," Autumn said slowly. "Even when I knew that Jo was their prime suspect."

I gave her a kind smile. "It was a remote possibility but one we needed to consider, nonetheless."

Autumn resumed walking toward where the parkour class was already gathering. "I can't blame you for that. Honestly. And that is what makes you two such great detectives. Every possibility is a viable one." She tossed us a smile. "But for the record, you two are my favorite people in this town, and I'd never let you take the fall for someone else. Heck, even if you had done it, I wouldn't have turned you in."

I gave Dottie a knowing smile. "See? I told you she was one of the good ones."

"I never said otherwise," she said, her gaze moving to Autumn. "It was Jo who said we should follow you."

I knew I shouldn't tease Dottie this way, but it was so fun to see her riled up. "You did say that good people can do terrible things."

"And they can," she said. "Look at Peter as a prime example."

Autumn merely laughed. "I'm not mad at you two, so no need to turn on each other. You should be more concerned that Coach David has asked Isaac to go through the required training to certify as an assistant coach. Isaac is awesome at everything he does because he's so driven, and I worry he'll expect the same of us."

She said this just as we approached the gathering class, and Isaac happened to overhear her. He turned.

"Thanks for the compliment, but I politely declined David's offer. As much as I enjoy the challenges of parkour, I can't afford to be splitting my attention. Not with the biggest surfing competition of the decade coming to Starlight Ridge. And if Bryce Carlton thinks he's going to win this one, then he's sorely mistaken."

I sensed a bitterness in Isaac's words I'd never heard before.

"Who is Bryce Carlton?" I asked. It was an innocent enough question, but from the way Autumn was looking at me—warning in her eyes—it had been the wrong one.

Isaac's expression darkened. "Only the most over-hyped, conceited surfer in the world. It's been rumored that he cheats, and I wouldn't doubt it. He should not have the ranking he does if talent is anything to go by. No one has been able to prove it, though."

"He's Australian," Autumn whispered. "Beautiful accent."

Isaac heard her and scowled. "He uses that accent as a weapon."

Coach David interrupted, calling for class to start. He spotted us at the edge of the group and walked over.

"I've had to go four weeks without a second assistant coach, and this guy says he isn't interested," David said, giving Isaac an amused smile, completely oblivious to the dark mood that had settled over us. "I could use your help to convince him that we're lost without his expertise."

I returned Coach David's smile, since it didn't look like Isaac would anytime soon. "It sounds like he has other things on his mind. When is this big surfing competition happening?"

"Six months," Isaac answered. "Right at the end of tourist season. Certifying to be a parkour assistant coach would take all of my time up until then." He glanced at the coach. "Sorry, David. Maybe after I demolish Bryce, then we can talk."

Coach David shrugged. "You know we'll all be cheering for you—you deserve this win. But I can't hold the coaching position for you. By that time, Jo will be ready to lead our advanced class."

Heat rushed up my neck. "You really think so?"

I knew Coach David was just being nice. But part of me hoped he wasn't—that he really had seen something that even I hadn't seen in myself.

David's eyes crinkled in amusement. "Let's get you back on the balance bar. You master that, you can master anything."

I stood a little straighter, my heart beating slightly faster than it should. "I'll conquer that balance bar. You watch." I paused. "But could I have that extra support you promised me? You know, just at the beginning while I'm getting the hang of it."

Now that I knew 'extra support' meant holding hands with the coach, I saw no downside. I'd set aside my pride, and I was ready to tackle anything Coach David sent my way.

Unless his next assistant coach turned out to be a murderer as well. That I could do without.

"Of course. I can give you all the support you need," David said with a smile. The kind that made all the other women in the class glare at me.

I loved parkour.

Isaac ran a hand through his hair. "I hope Jo does get that coaching position. Honestly, this will be the last class I attend until after the competition. I can't risk injuring myself—not with so much on the line. Bryce Carlton will never be able to look at those waves the same way again."

The fierceness in his voice—this wasn't just a surfing competition for Isaac. Something had happened in the past between those two, and this was personal.

I hoped for Bryce's sake that he saw it as such. Because I had a feeling things were going to get messy.

The End

CHOOSE YOUR OWN ADVENTURE: MYSTERY OR ROMANCE

MADDIE SWALLOWS MYSTERIES:

New Mexican Cozy Mystery

Dead Before Dinner

Dead Upon Arrival

Dead Before I Do

Dead Among Stars

Dead by Design

Dead in the Dark

Dead Without a Hitch

SEASIDE FRENCH PATISSERIE MYSTERIES

Death and Dacquoise

Poison and Pudding

BORROWING AMOR: New Mexican Romance

Borrowing Amor

Borrowing Love

Borrowing a Fiancé

Borrowing a Billionaire

Borrowing Kisses

Borrowing Second Chances

STARLIGHT RIDGE: Beach Romance

Diving into Love

Resisting Love

Starlight Love

Building on Love

Winning his Love

Returning to Love

Fearless Love

ABOUT THE AUTHOR

Kat Bellemore is the author of both the Borrowing Amor small town romance series and the Maddie Swallows cozy mystery series. Deciding to have New Mexico as the setting for these series was an easy choice, considering its amazing sunsets, blue skies and tasty green chile. That, and she currently lives there with her husband and two cute kids. They hope to one day add a dog to the family, but for now, the native animals of the desert will have to do. Though, Kat wouldn't mind ridding the world of scorpions and centipedes. They're just mean.

You can visit Kat at www.kat-bellemore.com.